AQUARIUMS

AQUARIUMS

J.D. Kurtness

Translated by
Pablo Strauss

RARE
MACHINES

Translation © copyright by Dundurn Press, 2022
Published by Dundurn Press Limited under arrangement with Les editions L'instant même, Longueuil,
QC, Canada. ALL RIGHTS RESERVED
Originally published as *Aquariums*, L'instant même, 2019

Publisher and Acquiring editor: Scott Fraser | Editor: Diane Young
Cover designer: Laura Boyle | Cover image: istock.com/Grafissimo

Library and Archives Canada Cataloguing in Publication

Title: Aquariums / J.D. Kurtness ; translated by Pablo Strauss.
Other titles: Aquariums. English
Names: Kurtness, J. D., 1981- author. | Strauss, Pablo, translator.
Description: Translation of: Aquariums.
Identifiers: Canadiana (print) 20210252995 | Canadiana (ebook) 20210253010 | ISBN 9781459747760
  (softcover) | ISBN 9781459747777 (PDF) | ISBN 9781459747784 (EPUB)
Classification: LCC PS8621.U785 A6813 2022 | DDC C843/.6—dc23

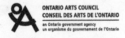

We acknowledge the support of the Canada Council for the Arts and the Ontario Arts Council for our
publishing program. We also acknowledge the financial support of the Government of Ontario, through the
Ontario Book Publishing Tax Credit and Ontario Creates, and the Government of Canada.

Care has been taken to trace the ownership of copyright material used in this book. The author and the
publisher welcome any information enabling them to rectify any references or credits in subsequent
editions.

The publisher is not responsible for websites or their content unless they are owned by the publisher.

Printed and bound in Canada.

Rare Machines, an imprint of Dundurn Press
1382 Queen Street East
Toronto, Ontario, Canada M4L 1C9
dundurn.com, @dundurnpress

Then God said, "Let Us make mankind in Our image, according to Our likeness; let them have dominion over the fish of the sea, over the birds of the air, and over the cattle, over all the earth and over every creeping thing that creeps on the earth." So God created mankind in His own image; in the image of God He created them; male and female He created them. And God blessed them, and God said unto them, "Be fruitful, and multiply, and replenish the earth, and subdue it: and have dominion over the fish of the sea, and over the fowl of the air, and over every living thing that moveth upon the earth."

— Genesis 1:26–27

1 The Right to Be Unhappy

HE AWAKES to a sky in that shade of blue that comes just before sunrise. The fire has burned down to a pile of glowing red embers. The others are still sleeping. He casts envious glances at the ones who share beds with women, a privilege he has let slip his grasp.

The pain of the tattoos was too much to bear. Yet the ritual ceremony got off to a good start. He was eager to see his body inscribed with his people's stories and entreaties to the gods for protection. It was a moment he'd visualized a thousand times before. He could picture a stoic figure impassive before the pain, see the blood, hear the hoarse voices chanting sacred songs. His face would be still as stone, his gaze determined, his self-control admired by one and all. He would go down in legend.

This flight of fancy was quashed in a matter of hours. He had been warned it would be the longest night of his life. He'd emerged from his trance, opened his eyes. The moon had only just climbed over the horizon. The very concept of dawn seemed inconceivable. His mouth had filled with saliva. Despite the heat, he was shivering violently. The chanting seemed to swell, as if his people could feel his faltering. But their voices, when they finally reached him, were muted. Their strength could scarcely scratch the surface of his weakness.

He pictured a broth with a layer of fat on top. Left out, the soup separates. That clear broth was him, unable to absorb the strength needed to face this trial. Above all, he had no thought for the consequences of his choice. This pain left him unable to think of other things. The suffering vanquished him, eclipsing all else. He begged for it to stop.

Despair wells up each time he remembers that he has been found wanting. His cheeks and back ache terribly. He can barely chew. He has to sleep on his stomach. At least the days are warm, as he can't imagine laying a garment over his torso. The slightest movement calls to mind his failure: he is not yet a man, not a full-fledged member of the tribe.

Though he is tall and broad and his penis grows hard at will, no woman would want to consort with a coward, a boy too weak to submit to the sacred ritual without flinching. He has brought shame upon his father. He's an object of mockery to his brothers and cousins. Even small children will tease him. Everything he endured this first time around will be in vain. He'll have to start again at the beginning. And he'll carry the double-markings as long as he lives, a silent reminder that he thought he was ready too soon. Now a cursory glance will make plain for all to see that he is vain, impatient, a poor judge of his own capacities. The hurried ones make the worst hunters.

His mother tries to console him. Perseverance also has its virtues. To submit to the ritual twice instead of once shows great courage. But what does she know? She's just a woman and hasn't had to submit to the men's ritual. What does she know of this dull, unrelenting pain that gnaws away at you for hours on end? With a smile in the corner of her eye, she answers, "I brought you into the world."

He doesn't dare admit that he fears failing again next time 'round. He must clear his mind, purify his spirit the way the shaman taught him. It's the only way he'll be able to push through the entire initiation rite. Pain is powerless against a strong mind. His people are known not only for physical prowess but also for their mental self-control. Long before their tattooed bodies appear on the horizon, their reputation has already terrorized the enemy. By the time they show themselves, defeat is a foregone conclusion.

His people have remedies for every malady save death itself. Their gods are listening and guiding them. The prophecies that visit them in dreams sooner or later come to pass. Is he worthy of bearing his ancestors' name?

He goes outside to think. The dwelling is stifling. He dislikes listening to his brother and Ita copulating. The sounds both excite and depress him. Outside, despite the chill in the air, a few shakes of his hand make him come. When he can concentrate again, he surveys the sky for signs of what the next few hours will bring.

He heads for the boats. Since he's awake anyway, he might as well make himself useful and go fishing. The mosquitoes don't bother him as he makes his way down the steep path to the water. That must mean his wounds have stopped bleeding. Despite the previous days' humiliation, he feels better. The aborted ritual left him nauseated and numb-legged. Those who complete the rite are entitled to rest, special salves that numb and fortify, tender glances from the womenfolk. He remembers the shaman's warm, dry hand on his forehead — a single, fleeting caress. Fading into exhaustion until he fell asleep. Awaking to dishonour.

The path wends its way through the rocks to the bottom of the cliff, where a thin strip of grey pebbles makes a smooth boat launch. Thousands of footsteps over several hundred generations have polished a path in the rock. He wonders how many of his predecessors trod this path with heavy hearts. Could such a fate have been foreseen at birth? Had a toad entered the room where he drew his first breath? The signs are always there. It's we humans who choose to ignore them.

They should have tossed him over the cliff, as the southern tribes do with their deformed newborns. All these stories are good for is scaring the children. Why, then, do they now creep in to cloud his mind? He has to pull himself together, apply the shaman's teachings, push away these harmful thoughts.

He walks onto the beach. The water lies still, walled in by the cliffs. A perfect reflection of the landscape stretches all around him. He must take care: three false steps will be enough to lose his footing. The fjord is so deep no rope weighted with stone could ever be long enough to reach its bottom.

Stories about a giant who sleeps in these depths are told to strike terror in the hearts of the little ones. The tiniest pebble might wake him; a single stone tossed carelessly into the water could leave the clan without fish for weeks. If yanked from his slumber, the curious giant will seek to punish the culprit. At any time, a gigantic hand could breach the surface of the water, grab a boat, and snap it in two like a tinder stick, squashing its unfortunate occupants like ripe fruit. This superstition has proven tenacious, and dropping anything heavy enough to sink is still considered a bad omen.

Such dark thoughts rarely come, but when they do, they're troubling. To pluck up his courage, he hurls a few rocks out into the water, using all his strength. Then he grabs canoe and oar, slides out onto the water. Of course, nothing moves. He paddles toward the mouth of the fjord, where the ocean spreads out as far as the eye can see.

It's going to be a beautiful day. A perfect day for fishing. The wind cuts scarcely a ripple in the water's vast expanse. Calm finds the wounded boy again. He wonders where the gods would lead him if he chose to paddle straight out into open water and never turn back. The fresh air numbs his hands and skin swollen from recent injuries.

When the coastline turns from green to blue — the blue of distance — he stops to ready his fishing gear. The only sounds are small waves lapping against the side of the boat and the breathing of porpoises in the distance. The sun climbs over the horizon. The boy is busy tying his knot when a loud crash tears through the air. Dry claps like thunder, then the breathing of what must be a colossal creature. For a moment he thinks it must be the giant. An irrational fear paralyzes him.

What he sees is more extraordinary still. A fantastical creature, black as night and pink as the sole of a baby's foot, is thrashing around in the surf just a hundred oar-strokes away. It dawns on him that what he's watching is not one creature but two. The whale has a head shaped like a log. The powerful breathing he heard is hers. Her jaw is clamped on the trunk and the arrow-striped tail of a headless creature with long snakelike arms. He counts eight of these appendages, but who could say for sure in this tumult? The many arms clutch the sperm whale's head with prodigious force. They even seem to be searching for the creature's blowhole and eyes and leave large circular wounds in their wake.

Blood pearls on the whale's torn skin; still, it refuses to yield. The enemies spin around in the spume under the boy's bewildered gaze. He has never seen a squid, much less a giant squid. The spectacle unfolding before his eyes has never been seen in living memory: a bloody fight to the death between two creatures from another world. As the sun climbs into a sky still graced with a pale crescent moon, the pearly pink of the squid reminds him of human flesh. The metallic scent of blood fills the air. Gulls flock by the hundreds, adding a new dimension to the din with their shrill squawks. The whale lets out a new salvo that rattles the boy's ribcage. The squid's trunk has been sectioned, but its tentacles flail on.

Then it's over. A few bobbing hunks of flesh drift toward the canoe. They are all that remains of this remarkable event. The water regains its oily sheen. The sun has not yet shed its orangey morning appearance. The boy has just one thought: *No one is going to believe me.*

My first memory is a fantasy: I'm thigh-deep in a layer of flour that stretches to the horizon. It's a pillowy world of white, dampening all sound. Solitude.

In my fantasy, I get to roll around in this flour for all eternity. I can see my compact four-year-old body, my underwear, my fine hair, and nothing else. It's a small heaven made for me alone, a thousand miles from that other dimension overcrowded with pious people I've never met, strolling along on the clouds. For a moment I swim, suspended in my desert of flour. It's softer than silk.

I return to this fantasy whenever I'm alone and before I fall asleep and again when I wake up. Whenever they leave me alone, basically. As soon as I get the chance, I dive right into this powdery realm of imagination. I become a worm, as tiny as a grain of rice, and tuck myself away in a bag in the back of the cupboard.

My mother dies. I'm not surprised. I've had time to get used to the idea. She was sick. One day she's there, loudly emptying the dishwasher; then she's in the hospital, and then comes the funeral home. I know it took her four months to die. That's what the grownups say anyway. But the mom I knew had already been gone for a long time. I'll never again visit that room with the light-blue paint and the machines. That frail body in the centre of the bed. That naked skull, those sunken eyes surrounded by purplish circles. The acrid smell of her medication. Where is she now, the smiling woman I see holding a baby in that photo in the kitchen hallway? I overhear someone telling my father I'm already done mourning.

I emerge from my white haze to find my father crying. We're in the car. He's driving; I'm strapped into my car seat in the back. I come out of my inner world and listen to the strange sounds he's making. My woollen tights are uncomfortable, and the label on my dress scratches my neck. It's cold in the car. It's raining. My new shoes are covered in mud. I was careful, but I wanted to throw a handful of earth on the coffin, to be like the others. I fight off the urge to wipe my hand clean on my clothes. It stays dirty.

We're parked in front of our house. I wait in silence for my father to pull himself together and come help me get unbuckled. Then I'll be able to take off my shoes, wash my hands, change my clothes, and watch TV.

My favourite toy at five is a miniature blue-and-yellow stethoscope. It's part of a medical kit, a set of scientific instruments that rest, each in its assigned place, inside a beige plastic case. I check the heart rate of everything: the floor, the walls, the cat, the dogs, my legs, my hands, my chest, my head. I check the ground to hear the earthworms wriggling beneath the surface.

I check the trees to hear the sap flowing, but the little scratches I hear are birds walking along the upper branches. I press the stethoscope's drum on our appliances and our doors. My favourite test subject is, of course, my father. And I have to face facts. A broken heart beats exactly like an unbroken one.

I decide I'm going to be a veterinarian. I make bandages for my stuffed toys out of rags and fashion an IV drip with drinking straws that draw from an apple juice bottle filled with water. I care for my dolls as best I can. They cough. They give birth. They catch the flu, cancer, chicken pox, cystic fibrosis. I pat them on the back for minutes on end so they can expel their secretions. They get better.

I start kindergarten at the same time as my neighbour. Valérie Lagueux has brown hair and is a full head taller than me. I spend a lot of time at her house after school, waiting for my dad to get home. But I don't really like it at the Lagueux's house. They have too much stuff. It feels as if all the furniture in the house is conspiring to target my shinbones with its sharp corners. Valérie's mom is constantly angry, and she snaps at us. Everything we do seems to annoy her. She's constantly asking us to go play outside so she can do the cleaning. And she never lets me take her heart rate. Maybe she doesn't want me to find out that she doesn't have one?

Mrs. Lagueux is a nurse. I imagine her ripping out IV drips, pressing down hard on patients' bruises, shaking them, yelling at them. A scary thought occurs to me. What if all nurses are like this the second visitors leave the hospital room? What hell did my mom have to go through? I can't ask my father, because talking about my mother makes him sad, and I hate seeing him cry.

Valérie doesn't seem bothered by her mother's attitude. The same goes for her little sister. Andréanne is only sixteen months old — still a baby, really — but I don't like her. She wears glasses that give her fish eyes, slobbers copiously, and eats dirt that collects with the uneaten bits of food on her chin and cheeks, forming little crusts. She's got a perpetually snotty nose. She may not talk yet, but she sure screams, staring right at you, with her mouth agape. And Valérie and I are the ones who get stuck playing with her and looking after her. I think she might have a mental disability, but don't dare ask. Thank God I'm an only child. No one gets to choose their siblings.

Mr. Lagueux works a lot, just like my dad. I leave when he gets home. He has a Mister Potato Head moustache, black hair, and pale white skin, even in summer. He usually wears a green tie. He's very tall and smells like perfume, more strongly than a woman even. The air in Valérie's parents' room is saturated with it. When I get back home, I sometimes feel like the scent has infused me as well. Mr. Lagueux also has hair plugs. Sad, lonely hairs have been sown in rows like saplings, from his forehead over the top of his skull. They gleam under the kitchen ceiling's halogen bulbs.

When I'm six, I ask my dad for a dog. The answer is no. No cat either. No rabbit, no parrot, no hamster. I swear up and down that I'll take care of my own pet, but nothing makes a difference. I'm jealous of the boy whose mother comes to meet him every day after school with a black dog. When he gets off the school bus, the dog wags its tail. His mother tries to kiss him, but he pushes her away in annoyance. I must make a weird face as I watch them, because Valérie's convinced I want to go out with him. Maybe I do. I mean, just to play with that dog. And get a closer look at this woman who caresses her son's neck with her thumb.

Reading, counting, learning new things? Easy-peasy. Valérie resents me and calls me a nerd. I tell her she just has to concentrate. That's the secret: you just have to look straight ahead to keep an eye on what's happening and listen to the teacher's explanations. It's beyond me how anyone could fail to get this or forget what the teacher told us just the day before. When I ask my dad, he tells me not to be mean to my classmates. I do my homework on the bus and let Valérie copy it. I always make a few mistakes, on purpose, and then correct them once I get home.

All through primary school, my dad isn't home much. And when he is, he's tired. We're getting by, one way or another, but he knows he should be more present. And he feels guilty. He wants to send me to boarding school. That would mean going away to a new school, since the one in our small town doesn't take boarders. The one in the city won't have me because I'm too young. My dad tries telling them I'm mature for my age, and I'd be better off there than here with him. Nothing doing. Boarders have to be at least eleven. No exceptions. In the meantime, he'll just have to keep working the same long hours. Money doesn't grow on trees. I get it. Maybe next year.

I'm ten, it's summer, and my dad has a new job travelling around, selling chemical products. Not the kinds of things you can just open a store and wait for people to come in and buy: it's more complicated. These chemicals are purchased in large quantities through supply contracts with governments and corporations. He lets me leaf through the catalogue that describes the full range of products his company makes.

My father is busy battling microbes, a foot soldier in an invisible war I'd never heard of up to then. In restaurants, schools, hospitals, shopping centres, and laboratories across the nation, everything has to be spotless. The same goes for prisons. Chemicals kill pathogens. Handled correctly, they're perfectly safe. Not one single microbe survives. The result is a healthy working environment. My father sells the world's most powerful cleansers. Watch out, viruses and bacteria! Here come the alkaline degreaser, antimicrobial hand soap, foaming sanitizer for organic containers, multisurface everyday cleaner, powerful urine neutralizer, and special cleaners for drains and grease traps. In the world of sanitation, these are the weapons of mass destruction. My father's briefcases hold samples as well. Our bathroom smells like a McDonald's washroom. Too bad school is finished: the other kids would have been impressed.

I pack my bags. I'll be spending this summer with my cousins. They live in a chestnut-brown brick house a few metres from my town's main street. There are no flowers or trees around it: just a little house in the middle of the lot, with some concrete steps between the asphalt driveway and the door. Clumps of yellowed grass grow in the sandy soil.

Aunt Élie is my dad's sister. Her husband Réjean drives a truck. When I was younger, I loved visiting them because their basement was a treasure trove. My aunt ran a little home daycare on weekdays, so they had every toy imaginable down there: bins of blocks, ponies, coloured pencils, doll clothes. Dozens of costumes and accessories, a carpentry workshop and kitchen, drawing tables that were just my height. As you went down their front hall, a staircase to the left led down to this wonderland. As far as I was concerned, my cousins were the luckiest kids in the universe.

When my aunt's sons got older, she shut down her daycare and opened a snack bar next to the campground. Now she spends her summers serving up fries, hot dogs, cheeseburgers, and poutine to the tourists who flock here to enjoy the beach. It's open from 11:00 a.m. to 11:00 p.m. My dad says that in just three months she can earn as much as in a full year looking after children. Summer is high season. The sand is warm, the lake a deep blue.

Yannick is thirteen, Kevin's twelve, and Laurent is eight. We all get along. It doesn't feel like anyone is in charge of me. My aunt works twelve hours a day, and my uncle isn't home much either. He picks up loads of massive logs deep in the forest and trucks them to the sawmill. Since Yan is the oldest child, he's in charge. He isn't very strict, as long as we don't do anything really stupid. We essentially do whatever we want.

Living with my cousins is a completely different world. I used to bathe every morning, but here the bathroom's usually busy. I'm reluctant to use the other, "grown-up" bathroom since you have to go through my aunt and uncle's bedroom. We're not allowed to go in there without knocking.

My cousins soak oatmeal in water as a skin treatment. Apparently bathing in oatmeal water keeps them from scratching themselves until they bleed. Their wrists and the insides of their elbows are rubbed raw from eczema. They even forego washing for days on end to keep from drying out their skin.

This oatmeal-soaking treatment leaves a brownish line in the bath. At first it grossed me out, but I stop noticing it soon enough. In our shared bathroom, the countertops and floors around the tub are littered with wet towels, toothpaste tubes, toothbrushes, shampoo bottles, combs, and creams. It's a far cry from the gleaming tile at my house.

I'd never really wondered what my favourite body care products were. I used whatever was around, meaning the same ones my dad used. Now I'm overwhelmed by choice. Aunt Élie was kind enough to suggest that I try hers. She says we have the same hair type. Her shampoo makes my hair much softer than the perennial Head & Shoulders at home. I love the merry chaos of this bathroom, where I shower with diminishing frequency.

Laurent, though he's the youngest, is the one who looks after me. I try to copy his attitude. Before I got here, I'd never so much as served myself a drink. I'd never used a sharp knife or shot an air rifle. Laurent doesn't let his older brothers push him around. He negotiates us time on the video-game console to play against each other, since otherwise Yan and Kev, who are vastly more experienced, will immediately blow us out of the water. The way they laugh when it happens is exasperating. At least Laurent gives me a chance when we go head-to-head. He also teaches me a few codes that, punched in at the right time, unleash merciless attacks that makes us scream with laughter.

Laurent makes our meals. It's weird deciding what we get to eat, and when, and even washing our own dishes. Aunt Élie buys us whatever we ask for at the grocery store. After that, we're on our own. Even when she does cook for us, we still have to portion it out and heat it up. Laurent's specialty is tomato-and-cheese soup. Pour one can of soup into a microwaveable bowl. Heat two minutes. Grate cheddar cheese on top. My young cousin is a patient, meticulous cook who doesn't let his eczema stand in the way of his dedication to his art.

We develop a little routine. I handle all the jobs that involve wetting your palms. When it's hot out, to avoid dirtying more dishes, we place the cans outside, on the concrete slab in front of the basement patio door. The canned spaghetti and meat balls are my favourite. Twenty minutes of full exposure to the sun is all it takes to heat them — okay, warm them — to perfection. Simply remove the lid by pulling the tab. Presto! Ready to eat.

Before I came here, I held certain naive beliefs. Cereal is only for breakfast. You can't drink strawberry soda in the morning. Wrong and wrong again! At my cousins', I discover that you can, in fact, gulp down anything, at any time of day, just because you feel like it. In the turquoise salad bowl, we mix a bunch of different cereals, all of which are strictly prohibited at my house because of their high sugar content. Laurent keeps some hidden in his room out of reach of his brothers and their ravenous friends. That way, when there's nothing left to eat, we always have the bottom of a bag for emergencies in the plastic bin where he keeps his socks. Since it's better with milk, we look for quarters in the couch cushions or take empty beer bottles back to the corner store for the deposit. Sometimes when we're just a little short, the clerk will let us leave with a carton of milk anyway. It depends who's working that day.

My cousins have a pool, but it's unusable because no one has time to take care of it. We're not allowed to swim when no adults are home anyway. Sometimes we ride our bikes down to the beach and pay the two-dollar admission fee, but that requires a serious stash of bottles and cans. We have to do a route with multiple streets, which takes time and involves discretion. It's not like we're the only ones out looking for pocket money. Every street is someone's turf. With two older brothers, Laurent has a defensive advantage. We can also barter with cigarettes swiped from Uncle Réjean. We make sure not to sneak more than one per day. At least, once we get to the campground on the beach, the fries are on the house.

Yannick has a brand-new bike with foot-pegs. He can even land tricks, just like the pros. Yannick's old bike got passed down to Kevin. Laurent has a new bike too, since nothing lasts long once Kevin gets his mitts on it. He's so strong and heavy that the cycle of handing down from brother to brother stops with him. I use Laurent's tiny BMX, the one he learned to ride on. That's fine. It reduces the likelihood of splitting my forehead on the handlebar. My jumps are getting faster and higher. The best part is landing: that perfect moment when my muscles and bones hold my body together, despite the shock of impact.

The backyard opens onto a huge vacant lot criss-crossed with tracks from four-wheelers. We got our hands on a rusty car hood. As long as you have enough momentum, it's perfect for jumping high and far. Lots of neighbourhood kids have started coming around to try their luck. Pieces of playground equipment are scattered around the lot, their pastel colours faded by the elements. These also became part of our race course. Three jujubes say Kev can't jump all the way to the Smurf. My personal record is landing next to Snow White without breaking my neck. Marc-André, Kevin's best friend, wasn't so lucky. What a wipeout! He caught the handlebar square in the face, lost a tooth, and was bleeding bad. Now he spits water through the hole constantly. It's his party trick.

We can all feel summer drawing to an end. The air is getting cooler. I've grown accustomed to sleeping in my bunk bed, above Laurent. At first, I had a hard time getting to sleep, but now I'd never go back. Laying there with nothing but a sheet beneath me and blankets above is way more comfortable than having a second sheet pinning me to the bed, like a dead butterfly. I much prefer being rolled up in two or three light blankets. No one here forces me to make my bed.

The linoleum in the basement stays cool no matter how hot it gets outside. There's the room I share with Laurent, and also Yannick and Kevin's rooms, and an open space that doubles as living room and playroom. This "basement" isn't actually underground, because the house is built on a slope. The patio door of the main room opens onto the backyard. We can watch the comings and goings of all the people who take the shortcut through the empty lot instead of staying on the road.

Very early one morning, a gang of teenagers shows up and steals our car hood. They also kick around our old toys. I even see one of them peeing on our log playhouse. With his dad's saw, Kevin had cut out a second door where the pretend fireplace used to be. Our game was to ride through the playhouse at full speed, without snagging your handlebar or banging your head. I don't kick up a fuss when I see them. Even drunk, these teenagers are stronger than us. They've got us outnumbered too. And there's no need to encourage Yannick, who's just looking for an excuse to pull out his knife.

My cousins and I watch a lot of TV. The only time I miss being home with my dad is when they watch porn movies. Kevin's friend Marc-André brings over VHS tapes he "borrows" from his dad. On those afternoons, not even Laurent

wants to play with me. At first, I tried to put on a brave face and watch them all the way through, but after a few minutes I felt sick to my stomach. It was the same feeling I got watching Andréanne eat dirt. The boys just laughed at me, but I don't care. I miss my stethoscopes. And Valérie's Barbies. At least the boys don't watch those movies too often. The ones where everyone shoots each other are just so much funnier.

Not long before I go back to my dad's, a miracle occurs. My uncle comes to pick us up, and we all pile into his burgundy Chrysler. It's not a long drive to the hospital, just ten minutes. My cousins are silent. We go up to the third floor, where my aunt is resting. In a plastic bassinet beside her lies fidgeting the most beautiful thing I've seen in my life. William weighs eight pounds, two ounces. His tiny nails can scratch you for real. I'm fascinated by his little belly button, with a big clip attached and what's left of the umbilical cord. They let me hold him. I run my lips over his little downy head, which has been gently misshapen by the birth. He falls asleep on me, even though my cousins are noisy as hell.

I go back to school a week later than the rest of the kids in town. My dad is coming to pick me up and take me home in three days. I try to make myself useful, to not be a burden, even though my aunt doesn't seem to mind having me around. She says I'm the little girl she'll never have.

I help my uncle build a shed. He thinks it'll be a place for the boys to make out with their girlfriends one day. It's a stretch for me to imagine any girl wanting to kiss my cousins with their eczema-ravaged skin and little purple penises. I mean, they're nothing like the handsome, buff guys in the skin flicks.

I'll miss them, with their smell of cortisone ointment and ketchup chips. I go out on my bike by myself and look back at the house. There it stands, all alone — so normal, so familiar. The everyday exterior camouflages the fact that, inside, we live like royalty.

2 In the Beginning

THE UMBILICAL cord gives out and the placenta begins its slow drift in a cloud of blood. A whale calf draws its first breath. The glacial air forces open the lungs. It's a brutal shock. Her mother is there, with warm milk and soft caresses. The newborn's aunts and cousins swim all around, exhilarated by this event and the risks it brings.

For these females, each birth is a moment of triumph and concern. Luckily, the pod of Orcas is still far away. The pack ice is only just beginning to crack. The calf's first weeks will be peaceful. So long as they keep track of the polynyas, they'll be able to breathe easy.

It's time to move on from here. The calf is now strong enough to swim a few kilometres.

• • •

An odour — suffusing his every pore, at once pungent and delicious: food. The sensation strikes him in the emptiness, waking him from his deep state of rest. His pulse quickens. Powerful tail strokes propel him slowly forward. The shark swims like this for three hours.

Muffled cracking sounds from the surface grow closer. Their vibrations envelop the shark's body in a familiar caress, heightening in intensity as the water pressure drops.

His muscles scarcely contract. His dark mass slips toward the surface, a few metres higher with each passing minute. Every forward movement costs him precious energy. Opportunities to feed are rare.

A shadow among shadows, he glides like a ray between the currents. Water this frigid should by all rights be frozen. Only the salt, tides, and pressure have kept it liquid.

Above, the pack ice sings. Its cracking sends waves of sound into a glacial darkness, small shocks that stimulate the shark's every nerve. There is life up here as well. A whole world, travelling at an unimaginable speed, suffocating in its heat and light.

Before, the shark would stare at the shimmering layer of thick ice: green or blue in bright light, orange and pink as the sun slipped over the horizon. The coming of night revealed thousands of multicoloured, glimmering electric creatures. He can still feel their teeming presence, even if he can no longer see them.

Other sharks begin their ascent to the surface. Copepods have attached themselves to each of their eyes. The parasites spin around, mirroring the movements of their giant hosts. No light reaches down to these depths. Only on the rare occasions when they rise to the surface in search of a meal do the sharks experience light. Sooner or later rotting corpses sink.

His eyes have been eaten by the copepods. They're useless now. Even when he brushes his snout up against the limits of the known world, he sees only blackness. After two hundred years of blindness, a hazy memory of light remains, lodged in the deep centre of his brain.

The shark locates the feast. The whales are already far away. He'll be first to eat, a rare privilege. He bites off hunks of fresh, dense meat. Hunger sated, he lets himself sink gently back down toward the ocean floor to wait once more.

I turned eleven at the end of that summer, and I grew a lot. Gained weight, got a tan. Bleached by the sun, my hair went from the colour of wheat to an almost white blond. My dad made a funny face when he came to pick me up. He looked pale. While I was stuffing my face with hot dogs at the beach and perfecting my technique for BMX jumps, he'd been lugging sample cases all over the U.S. and Western Europe. It didn't exactly leave him time to play outside.

I'd changed since he last saw me. My clothes didn't fit any more, especially my pants, so I was wearing hand-me-downs. Black shorts with a fluorescent green pattern, red-and-blue tank tops, jeans frayed at the knees and the ass. Clothes that had survived Yannick's mild pyromania, Kevin's countless falls, and Laurent's culinary experiments. Wearing these clothes made me feel invincible, as if I had donned armour equipped with the most powerful protection of all — family. Laurent even gave me his old mittens so I'd be ready for winter. His grandmother had sewn him a new pair. When I asked what the sheepskin patches on the back of each one were for, he shot me a funny look, as if I'd asked him what bikes were for.

"For wiping your nose, duh! Bring them at Christmas, and we'll go skidooing."

My dad thought he'd found a great deal when he tracked down several pieces of my uniform second-hand. Too bad he'd bought the sizes I wore back in June, before he parked me at Élie and Réjean's for the summer. Obviously, there was no way he was going to drop me off at my new school on a Sunday night with a bunch of skin-tight polo shirts and skirts I could only zip halfway up. Since there wasn't much time, he had no choice but to buy me a bunch of new polo shirts, skirts, and shoes. And a gym strip, of course. We were going to spend an hour a week running around the gym, and the sky would surely fall unless we did it in navy blue shorts and a grey T-shirt with the school logo. It was dumb, but that's the way it was.

This is when it dawns on me that we're poor. The idea had never crossed my mind before. When my mom got sick and my dad had to look after her, it must have wreaked havoc on our finances. I guess Dad took his new job so we wouldn't lose our home. He must be attached to it for sentimental reasons; I sure hope it's not for my sake. A big empty house just depresses me. When people come to visit, the carpeting makes them sneeze. They're not used to the dust. The weeds are slowly invading the rock garden. The cupboards squeak when you open them. Even my bed seems smaller, shoved way to the back of my bedroom. My room is a still a little girl's room, frozen in time. It's high time to redecorate. Filling a bag with all the toys I don't play with and tossing them would make a good start.

My dad may be making more money now, but he's also away a lot. For me that means living with his sister and then heading off to boarding school 143 kilometres away, just to keep our neighbours from calling child protection services. I know perfectly well I could look after myself, especially after the highly educational weeks I've just spent at my aunt's. But that would be illegal.

I turned eleven just in time. In the past few months, we've narrowly avoided having our house repossessed. I saw envelopes labelled "FINAL NOTICE" on the kitchen counter. Heard my dad negotiating on the phone. Whenever he closes the door to the room he uses as an office, I know it's a bad sign. Our new financial situation means we can handle mortgage payments and school fees, but there's not much left over after the bills are paid. I decide that from now on, I'll be careful with money and look after myself.

I don't like being a boarder though. After living free and easy all summer, the rules at boarding school are hard to swallow. I get it: we need rules to structure community living for a group of teenage girls. But there sure seems to be an awful lot of them. Make your bed. Eat only at mealtimes. No food in the dormitories or in the study hall, where only whispering is tolerated. No speaking after curfew. Lights out at nine.

No going outside, except at set times. We even need a parent or guardian's express permission to leave the school grounds. And, of course, no boys!

For the first weeks, I'm in a state of shock. Accustomed to eating as soon as the first hunger pangs strike, my body struggles to wait for the allotted three meals at their fixed times. I get headaches and stomachaches, especially at night. I can feel my stomach digesting itself and a burning in my chest. When these pains wake me, the only remedy is to drink water to dilute the acidity. The bathroom is far away, the floor ice-cold. So I hold it in and develop a reputation as the girl who takes the longest pees every morning. I guess it's better than being the girl who pees her bed.

I think about food all the time. Yet they feed us well here. Every meal is balanced, with meat, starch, vegetables, and a square portion of that day's cake served in a tiny bowl. Tall glasses of milk are set out on the tables several minutes before we invade the dining hall. This room-temperature milk is my favourite part. By the time we sit down to eat, it's perfect — not too hot, not too cold. Being hungry all the time is ridiculous, but I don't want to bother my dad with small details.

The other girls are nice enough. It was more fun living with my cousins, but there's no way I can go back. Since William was born, my uncle and aunt have had their hands full with four kids in the family. I wonder if he cries at night. I don't call them to find out. Long-distance calls cost a fortune. And when it comes to using a phone, boarding school is like prison: everyone can listen in on your conversation.

The phone is in a little wooden closet, with a curtain for a door. The thing looks more like a confessional than a phone booth. It must have been put in sometime in the nineteenth century, around when Alexander Graham Bell was popularizing the invention. Talking on the phone isn't my style anyway. Or Laurent's, come to think of it. I could call my dad, if I wanted. His company gives him a cellphone, since he doesn't have a permanent office. I know the number, but we agreed I'd only use it for emergencies. He feels bad enough as it is. I don't want to lay on another layer of guilt with my moods.

I have to force myself not to think too much, because certain thoughts make me sad — my dad working to pay for a house no one lives in anymore, the framed photo of my mother and me hanging in the hallway, Valérie's little sister Andréanne starting Grade One at a special school. (I was right. She really does have special needs. Either that or she ate too much dirt? Maybe her dad's cologne melted her brain?)

Valérie's mad because I'm going to private school now — what she calls "rich girls' school." She says that since my house is sitting empty she and her friends are going to break in and throw a party. That I deserve to have my things stolen because I'm a traitor. I tell her that if they do, the police won't have to look too far to find the culprit. But I know she's bluffing. My father says she's just sad because she's lost her best friend. I had no idea I was Valérie's best friend.

At my new school, the sheets smell like bleach. Unlike the other kids, who put on their headphones and listen to music to put themselves to sleep, I listen to the beat of my own heart on my stethoscope. Whenever I get too lonely and might be tempted to make a call, the dark night and freezing-cold floor dissuade me from trying my luck with the phone booth.

There's a girl from Guatemala in my new class. She only just got to Canada, right in the middle of winter. We came back to school after Christmas break, and there was Pilar in the front row. Nobody talks to her. Of course, we collectively mumbled a polite "hello" at the teacher's insistence. But no more.

A tacit nonaggression pact is observed by all the boarders. There are only five of us eleven-year-olds. Gisèle Landry, Caroline Corriveau, and I, Émeraude Pic, are in one Grade Six class. Stéphanie Pilon and Marie Fauteux are in the other class. The other boarders are high-schoolers, and their classrooms are off in a different building. Though we spend evenings together in the common rooms, we still don't mix much with them.

The other boarders are no better off than me. Caroline lost her mother too. Hers had a stroke last winter and died suddenly. You can see she's still struggling with it. Not me. The idea that I don't have a mother anymore is a tender spot, but I've gotten used to it. That doesn't make me especially good at comforting other people though. Case in point: I told Caroline you could get used to pretty much anything. She just started crying. Hard. Her dad must be pretty dumb if he thinks he's helping his daughter to get over her loss more quickly by sending her away to boarding school.

Gisèle is the youngest of her siblings. She has three sisters and one brother, all of whom have already gone away to university, or on to some other stage of grown-up life. It feels like she was probably an accident. Her parents must figure they've done enough parenting for one lifetime and feel no guilt outsourcing Gisèle's care to our school.

Stéphanie lives in a town near mine. Her parents are adamant about giving her a private-school education. She's been crying every night since school started. She misses her friends. Even Caroline thinks she's laying it on a little thick. I mean, crying loud enough for everyone to hear you is just plain rude. Imposing your pain on others should be avoided at all costs. We can all hear her sobbing away, begging her mommy to come get her. The phone booth curtain can only hide so much.

Then there's Marie. She's the resident bad girl. Boarding school is basically her last chance before juvie. There are various rumours going around about her, but the only one that's true is that she's going to fail Grade Six. It's January, and she still can't get a handle on the stuff we learned in September. The worst part is that Marie's not actually stupid. She's just pretending, to piss off her parents. Bad marks are her way of fighting the system. It makes no sense, but she persists in not doing her homework and gives nonsense answers on her tests. I keep my distance because I can't understand why she'd be that way. She's the type who'll end up bound to a bed with leather straps.

We don't talk openly, but you still end up knowing everything about everyone at school. Living in close quarters will do that. When Marie saw a photo of my mom on my bedside table, she told me she could see the resemblance. Maybe, she suggested, that's why my dad didn't want to see me anymore? At least it's not because I was giving five-dollar blowjobs to buy mascara, like *some* people we know, I answered. That cracked her up, and she asked if we could be friends. I said no, but not to take it personally. I'm on a friendship strike for the year.

As boarders we enjoy a special, but not very desirable, status at school. We must be surrounded by some kind of doleful aura that makes the other kids ignore us. And we eye them enviously as they pack onto the yellow school buses at the end of the day. Others walk, often in clusters of five or six, because they live nearby. Some even get the royal treatment: a parent comes to pick them up. One thing is sure: no one lingers after the bell rings at three twenty. Pilar takes the Number Twenty-Six bus, which is always one of the first to leave, outside the school. She hobbles over to the bus and laboriously climbs its steps. Watching her becomes a little ritual for me. I have to make sure Pilar gets on her bus okay before I can relax.

It's a relief to no longer be the new girl. And I don't even have to talk to the *new* new girl. We're boarders; no one expects us to. That's the popular girls' job. They're the arbiters of social status. Overall, the group dynamics here are much more complex than at my old school, which only had one class per grade. Everyone knew each other. It also feels weird to be living and going to school with only girls. As if to make up for it, they spend far too much time talking about boys. I can't help wondering what Pilar thinks of all this. She definitely won't be part of the popular clique. You have to be on at least one school sports team for that — not an option for me since it involves an extra fee. Pilar has an even better excuse: she's got a club foot. She limps like an old woman. It's caused by an illness she had when she was a baby. I guess it must be true: she really does come from the developing world.

Gisèle got tons of Christmas presents. That's the upside of having a big family. One of her sisters knitted her a scarf. Another bought her a bunch of CDs. We pass around the Discman her parents got her, taking turns listening. I've managed to convince her that music sounds better with both headphones, even if it's all the rage to sit next to your friend with one each. I like Gisèle because nothing seems to faze her. She never complains.

Marie is jealous. As far as she's concerned, my "friendship strike" was a pack of lies. Well, it *was* true at the time — I just changed my mind. It's like my aunt Élie used to say: only fools and dead men never change their minds. I can imagine a future when we've all grown older. I'll visit Marie between two rounds of her electroshock therapy, bring her a bouquet of daisies and some chocolate, and show her my Nobel Prize in Medicine. I'll win for being the one who finally eradicated germs, for good. But I won't be able to do anything about her addled brain.

Music is something I'd never really paid much attention to before. Gisèle lends me her things without a second's hesitation, and that makes me proud. I guess I'm one of those people you can trust. Her sister's albums are amazing. There's one group I hated at first, but now they're my favourite. They sing in English, so I decide to translate one of their songs.

The lyrics are in the liner notes. I copy out every song and memorize the words. Original English on the left-hand page; my translation on the right. It's strangely soothing. Only now do I understand Stéphanie, who chases her sorrows by writing out her favourite actor's name in huge letters. Her agenda is filled with multicoloured incantations consisting of his name adorned with hearts and stars. When she isn't doing her homework, Stéphanie is figuring out new ways to write out her idol's name. I'm impressed by her extreme dedication. And beyond that, her perseverance, even with everyone laughing at her and telling her she has no chance of ever meeting the man in person. I mean, she's twelve years old, doesn't speak English, and shows no signs of ever being pretty enough to land a role in Hollywood.

My Christmas holidays were incredible. My dad spent a full ten days with me. He even came to pick me up at school on December 22. I saw my cousins, and we went skidooing just like they'd promised we would. William has doubled in size. He's a big, heavy, fidgety child. You have to hold on to him tightly now, or he'll wiggle out of your grasp and end up on the ground. And his laugh has gotten super loud. Laurent gave me a YA novel. I'd already read it, but I didn't tell him, or let him know that I read grown-up novels now. I gave him a recipe book. I'd chosen all the recipes I thought he'd like in the cookbooks they had in the town library. Then I copied them out into a notebook, like I did with the song lyrics. He looked happy.

The best present of all was from my dad though: a real professional microscope, just like the ones scientists use. It's a heavy instrument in a white case with black screws. The lenses have chrome housings. My dad's company was getting rid of them because they bought newer models. It even came with a bunch of replacement bulbs and a special oil to use with the most powerful settings.

It works super well. You have to turn a screw a bunch of times to adjust the lenses, and the focus is incredibly accurate. I was able to bring it into the dormitory. Everyone knows it's mine. It's not like anyone else cares about it. I don't show the other girls the mites I examine — that might unleash a panic, maybe even get my microscope taken away. I can't imagine a more precious possession. It can enlarge up to eight hundred times. It turns out that just about anything is fascinating if you just cut off a slice and place it on a glass tray.

Caroline brings me lichen saturated with creek water. You should see the water bears. Amazing! It's the first time I've seen them in real life, not on TV. Tardigrades are the best. They've got cute little feet and mouths like a plastic spout, and totally look like jujubes. They're beautiful. I look at my sample as I listen to my favourite song on one of the albums I borrowed from Gisèle. A robot is reciting a wonderful, yet terrible, poem while these transparent creatures dance to their very own rhythm right before my eyes.

3 The Mantle of the Earth

ON APRIL 5, 1815, the Mount Tambora volcano erupts. For days on end, the volcano spews out millions of tons of lava, ash, and stone over the island of Sumbawa in the Indonesian Archipelago. The rare survivors' accounts describe a cloud of debris so dense it completely blocks out the light of the sun for three days. Those not killed instantly perish slowly of hunger. For the next five years, within a three-hundred-mile radius, the earth is barren.

The blast has repercussions far beyond the region. In many parts of the northern hemisphere, 1816 is the "year with no summer." The rains of ash released by Mount Tambora block out the sun. A cold, hard rain falls over Europe relentlessly.

Also in 1816, Leonas is born.

The small church is packed. Many people would have happily stayed warm and cozy in their homes, but no one likes to imagine burning in hell or being stuck in purgatory for all eternity. Already they are waiting in vain for a spring that never seems to arrive; no one wants to risk further offending the creator. Halfway through the service, during the reading from Saint Paul's Second Epistle to the Corinthians, the rain starts up again. The story of Jesus and the clay vessels comes from a time when men and women roamed free. Since casting aside their worldly borrowings to follow the teachings of Christ, they walk on light feet. The peasants assembled here envision their saviour wearing sandals, in a landscape where the fruit trees grow wild. The sun shines on his light-coloured tunic. This garment, so perfectly suited to the Mediterranean climate, keeps him cool by day and warm at night — nothing like the damp, smelly wool overcoats worn by those who have gathered in this drafty nave. Their clogs are covered with lumps of cold mud. Water seeps into their already-damp socks. The biblical story brings comfort, transporting the more attentive ones to another world. It also keeps their hunger at bay. No one eats before Sunday mass in normal times, let alone during Lent. As if their cellars weren't bare anyway. They avidly await the sowing season. The second this evil rain stops falling, all will be out in the fields.

Though he is small and dirty, the man delivering the sermon possesses great warmth. He truly loves his hardworking, meek flock. They cannot easily see themselves in this sermon. Only through divine grace is the Latin language accessible. Up in the pulpit, the priest provides a gloss: "You see, these bearded men in tunics didn't have it easy either. At every moment they stared death in the eye, faced the prospect of nails driven into their palms and feet or even being crucified upside down. You may not be basking in the Judean sun feasting on lamb — but at least you are free. Through these men's sacrifice, and in exchange for virtuous living, you have been granted the gift of faith, the word of God, and the possibility of eternal life."

This is the part in the sermon when their attention always wanders. A polite silence fills the room. These peasants have heard this uplifting speech about the beauty of the Baltic Sea and the importance of fighting the Russian enemy a thousand times before. You can hear them coughing.

The Eucharist brings an uptick in enthusiasm. The ceremony is almost over. A final blessing and they will at last be able to push open the big wooden door. It's snowing. They are visibly disheartened. Yet a certain excitement, undampened by the weather, takes hold of the first worshippers to pass through the door. A basket has been laid out on the third step, exposed to the elements assailing the heart of the village. Inside: the crumpled face of a newborn, so pale in its swaddling bundle it could almost be dead. A strong smell rises from the basket. They stare, rapt, at the tiny grey body, until it is rocked by a powerful hiccup. The people spring into action. A motherless foundling. The infant is taken to the presbytery. The priest decides: the butcher's wife will nurse it. She lost her youngest to the whooping cough. Now God has delivered her a gift, this orphan. He baptises him Leonas. A pope's name. Amen.

Despite these beginnings, Leo's first months are peaceful. His adoptive mother loves his calm, his smiles, his warm compact body. Leo isn't like other infants. He doesn't cry. If he is forgotten for a few hours, he merely drinks more greedily than usual. This forbearance is a source of fascination and envy to the other parents. The lean harvests, cold weather, and harsh winter that mark the first year of his life don't ruffle his serene disposition. His mother's thin milk provides nourishment, but Leo remains short and chunky. He has no sense that his grandfather's death is a blessing: one less mouth to feed, a few more quarters of meat. A light coffin.

Leo is precocious. Before he turns one, he is already walking. The year 1817 offers up a hesitant summer, but the harvest season finds the farmers singing in the field. In the hustle and bustle of work on the farm, Leo is forgotten out in the field not once but twice. The first time, they find him exactly where they left him, next to the sheep pen. A bad case of sunstroke will leave the skin on his cheeks peeling off for weeks. The second time, Leo follows his father one morning and falls asleep with the cows. It's a miracle he doesn't get trampled to death.

Perhaps his fondness for animals saves him. Leo's love runs much deeper than mere care for a job well done. He can spend hours out in the fields just admiring the animals. He never hits the dogs or tortures the cats, doesn't throw stones at any creature great or small, or yank off the feet of reptiles or insects. When the others play these games, he stands aside.

He stoically watches his father slaughtering and butchering. Soon he'll learn to dispatch these tasks with unmatched efficiency. It angers Leo when one of his brothers botches a killing, pointlessly prolonging the animal's suffering. At a glance, he can tell the time needed to render an animal and the weight of meat it will yield. It's said he can even sniff out the meat's quality. He claims scared animals taste bad.

His father doesn't know what to do with this gentle but hot-tempered child. His movements are precise, his expression resigned. Leo doesn't grow tall, but he is sturdy and diligent. A model son, pride of his parents. Many of the villagers regret that they did not volunteer to take in the child, instead of letting the priest decide his fate. They'd love to have had such helpful offspring. But Leo belongs to no one. He was lost, as treasures sometimes are. The ones who didn't speak up would live forever with that mix of shame and sadness of those who fell silent at a critical juncture in their story.

At thirteen Leo falls in love. He and his father have taken the westbound road to the city, where his older brother, who never had the knack for butchering, is apprenticing as a brewer. It's a quieter, less bloody art. In a sign that he has taken to the trade, he's even started pestering his father to let him grow a few acres of hops.

As they near the port, Leo is drawn to the smell of the salty air. Then, in between the sails and the hulls, he catches a glimpse of sunlight dancing on the water. It's a shock, for he has never seen the sea. Bewitched, he walks straight toward it. His curious father has no choice but to follow. His youngest child is normally so serious. He so rarely lets himself get swept up in anything. Leo goes down to the docks and kneels on the ground. He is flabbergasted. After a few minutes, he gets up and embraces his adoptive father. He takes a deep breath, to drink in the man's ferrous, dried-blood scent one final time. His mind is made up. His father will walk home alone. Leo will sample a few of the new malts his brother has spent the last months working on. Then he'll go to sea.

Since he can't read, Leo has no way of knowing that the first ship he enlists on is named *St. Casimir's Glory*. Once aboard, all the most thankless jobs will be his. Scrubbing and swabbing every surface, coiling up wet ropes, climbing up to tie or untie knots, tasting the rations when their freshness is in doubt, emptying the chamber pots overboard, and more.

Leo finishes every task they throw at him without flinching. Other crew members may snigger and mock him, but not one lays a hand on him. He's free, adrift on the deep blue sea, cradled up in a hammock where sleep comes the moment his eyes close. His skin cracks in several places, rubbed raw by hard work and salt. Since his hands are usually frozen anyway, he scarcely feels the pain. And having blood under his nails is nothing new. After a few weeks, his hands are as calloused as the rest of the crew's. He doesn't suffer from seasickness, didn't know such a thing existed until someone new takes his place as the ship's Johnny-come-lately. This new hand spends the entire eleven hours of his short maiden voyage heaving over the side.

Their fishing expeditions are dreary and dangerous. Leo eyes the larger ships whose paths they cross in the open waters, far from the small docks where the fleet of fishing boats anchors. Never could he have imagined just how vast this world could be.

He often harks back to his brother and father's reactions when he told them he wished to go to sea. They were clearly both surprised and relieved. It smarts a little knowing his leaving has made their lot easier, but he was the third and last child. He knows all too well that they saw him more as a ticket to heaven than a son.

There was never any question of his taking over the family business, a role destined for legitimate heirs. Nor was there money to place a second apprentice in town. Although his adoptive mother still filled his bowl as high as those of the others, he had become a burden.

She always felt responsible for his small size. The cap he still wears will be her last gift to him. It's warm: she knitted it for him before he left for the city, worried he might catch cold on the long walk. He hasn't taken it off since. He would have liked to say goodbye, to thank her for bringing him up tough enough to rub his hands raw on the rigging without a word of complaint. His forbearance is a point of pride. Earning the older men's respect brought joy.

After two years on the *Casimir*, he convinces the captain of a large merchant ship to take him on. The *Dancing Gull* is an impressive wood-and-iron three-master with heavy blue sails. Leo now has regular pay. It's enough for a hot bath, fresh fruit, and a few pints when they drop anchor in exotic ports. He prefers these simple pleasures to following the rest of the crew to the brothels. Something about the lipsticked, pale-skinned, sneering women scares him a little. They cry out tall orders when he walks past their garishly lit establishments. He shoots them a smile and gets back to the ship, where he shares his meal with any mice brave enough to come pick the crumbs from between his fingers.

Exceptional times call for exceptional measures. I've been given permission to leave school for an evening in the middle of the week. It's a Wednesday, and I'm calmly finishing off my dessert, listening to Gisèle and Caroline rate the different Grade Nine teachers, when I get my period for the first time. We've been back from holidays for ten days, and they were finding the return to boarding-school life a hard pill to swallow.

But I'm glad to be back. It was a long rainy summer. My cousins were off camping in the States, and I spent most of my time watching TV and eating ham sandwiches. For my dad, it was business as usual, selling his chemicals. Last I heard, he was in Delaware.

Stéphanie's parents were the ones who picked me up for the start of classes. The crying fits have come and gone. She's now firmly ensconced in her Goth phase: dying her hair black, listening to the Cure. I can feel a boy's presence lurking behind this sudden metamorphosis. She's got a new name to decorate her notebooks.

Every one of Stéphanie's polo shirts is brand new. I'm trying to squeeze a few more months out of the ones I've had for three years now. They've worn to a noticeably duller sheen than those of the other girls. This town has hard water — not unfit for drinking, just hard enough to make clothing washed in it quickly lose its lustre. I have to be careful not to raise my arms, since the armpits are stained with hundreds of layers of deodorant and years of sweat that no washing can hope to remove. I should probably swallow my pride and ask some of the girls to hand me down their old clothes, but I just can't bring myself to do it. Maybe if I was really getting tormented. But people more or less leave me alone. And I keep my money problems to myself.

I'm chewing my last bite of carrot cake when I'm hit by stomach pains and cramps, followed by an unpleasant sensation of involuntarily wetting my panties. I explain the situation to the boarding school authorities, meaning Josée, the chiropractic student who's in charge of us from five to midnight on Mondays, Wednesdays, and Fridays. Out of a sense of female solidarity, Josée hands me a twenty and sends me to the nearest drugstore. She has to stay to watch the other girls and no, I can't take a friend. "Deal with it, Émeraude Pic!

I've rarely strayed outside the school walls. It's my first time walking the streets of the neighbourhood. I don't have far to go though — ten minutes max. Night falls, and I don't run into anyone on my way. Summer's almost over. I'm struggling to imagine the conversation coming up with my dad about my need for a "feminine allowance."

It may not be fair, but I resent him a little for not seeing this coming. I'm going to have an unpaid debt with Josée for this. Wow, there's a fabulous little father-daughter confab to look forward to!

Is my flow "heavy" or "light"? Am I more of a tampon- or sanitary-napkin type? With wings? For "active" women? I vaguely remember an ad with a bunch of cheerleaders wearing immaculate tight white pants, dancing with big smiles. Ladies: your athletic prowess and positive attitude can fuck right off. The very last thing I feel like doing right now is standing up in the middle of a crowded football stadium and doing a little dance. And I highly doubt that any type of feminine protection is going to change my mind.

As I head toward the till, I find myself in front of what must be the most bizarre sight of my admittedly short life. This being is clad entirely in white, in some sort of soft, full bodysuit, like a beekeeper's, except that where the face-covering should be there is instead a shield of mirrored glass that prevents anyone from seeing their face. Picture Lawrence of Arabia if he wore a welding helmet. Not one patch of skin is exposed. Cotton gloves cover this person's hands. It's twenty degrees Celsius outside.

You'd need to live in terror of the cold to rock a getup like that. The wearer is taller than me and busy chatting with his mother, who's standing beside him. He has the croaky voice of an adolescent male. They're having a friendly argument in the sunscreen section. For no reason I can name, as if pulled by some mysterious force, I find myself walking toward them. They stop dead and check me out. At any rate, the woman scopes me out, and I imagine the human rocket must be doing the same under his Halloween costume or cult robes. But what's gotten into me to make me approach them? I feel somehow naked in my worn-out sandals, shorts, and blouse. To cap it all off, I'm carrying twenty dollars of feminine hygiene products and a bottle of extra-strength Tylenol.

They must be used to the stares. After slightly awkward introductions, Henri (which turns out to be Lawrence of Arabia's given name) launches into an explanation of his serious allergy to sunlight. He's fourteen, like me, but unlike me hasn't felt the sun on his skin in over a decade. His cells lack the normal human capacity to repair themselves. Unless he wants to go out of his way to get cancer, he has to slather on sunscreen the second he goes outside — even if not one millimetre of his skin will be exposed to the deadly rays. Henri hands over a little card that describes his condition and gives the address of his website. He's raising money for a new helmet that would be less disruptive than his current model, letting him go out in daylight.

Our introductions would probably have gone over better if I didn't feel like my reproductive system was liquefying. I can't remember exactly what I said. But of course, I end up spending the entire evening, and then the night as well, thinking about Henri. I use the few remaining minutes before curfew to do a little internet research. I learn a new term: pigmented xeroderma. It's a life sentence. The website has an email address, a phone number, and a button you can click to make a donation. How awful to be unable to feel the sun on your skin. I mean, that's probably my greatest pleasure in life. In the Western world, this disease afflicts fewer than four people per million. Congratulations, Henri! You won the hard-luck lottery.

Henri answers all my questions patiently. Or if his patience does wear thin, I don't pick up on it. He writes me long stream-of-consciousness emails about being home-schooled by his mother. He was in a normal class before, but the logistics of that, and the ensuing panic attacks, eventually set him on a different course. Anti-UV filters had to be installed in every window of the school so the sun's rays wouldn't reach him. These windows remained locked at all times, because the sun's rays can filter through any available opening. It makes sense, since as dermatologists tell us, even staying in the shade without sunscreen entails risk. At Henri's house they've put in double doors. His doorway is an airlock: you have to make sure the first door is closed before opening the second. As even standard light bulbs emit hazardous rays, at Henri's they only use LEDs. And even then, he always wears sunglasses.

When Henri gets older, he won't get to party like every other young person in the world. Alcohol and drugs are toxic to all organisms, sure, but Henri's body lacks the ability to heal itself. If it weren't for all the precautions he takes, he'd already be dead. So he spends his days playing video games and surfing the internet. Even his CRT computer monitors have UV filters, which his mother has patiently cut out from window film.

I now know a disturbing number of things about Henri's private life, but I've still never seen his face. The one photo he's uploaded to his website isn't recent. Henri was a good-looking kid. Brown curly hair, brown eyes, full lips, a solid covering of freckles. Before the diagnosis, his parents thought the freckles were cute; after, they became alarming.

I'm pretty much obsessed with Henri. I can't believe I'm his only friend in the world. Over time, he gradually lost touch with all his classmates from back when he could still go to school. He wants to know whether my interest in him is purely scientific. Well, I guess it might be. But Henri doesn't mind. He finds me "entertaining."

Anyway, we're finally going to be able to hang out in person soon. I've gotten permission from both my dad and the school to spend a weekend at Henri's house. His mother approves. His father probably would too, if he hadn't left them right after Henri's diagnosis. A son, for him, meant someone you could take to the park on a sunny afternoon and play catch with. Against such a powerful idea, the actual Henri and his mother didn't stand a chance.

Henri lives close to school. I'd suspected as much, ever since I ran into them in the drugstore. He and his mother have a big grey brick house. It's almost six at night when I get there, and it's November so the sun has gone down. To my astonishment, Henri is waiting for me, sitting on the steps that climb his steeply sloped yard. He's not wearing his helmet.

When he smiles at me, I recognize the boy in the photo. Like the rest of his body, his face has thinned out. But I'd also say he's fattened up a little since the day we met in the drugstore. I'm right: he explains that his medication makes him gain weight. There are antidepressants and anti-anxiety pills.

The house smells wonderful. He and his mom have been cooking for me all afternoon. Even though no one has ever lavished this much attention on me, I pretend it's no big deal.

After dinner, we go for a walk. Henri has a cellphone and calls his mother every half hour to tell her where we are. He doesn't seem to mind having to check in like that. It's very late when we come home — almost midnight. They give me a big room to sleep in, with varnished wooden floors and an incredibly comfy bed.

When I get back to school Sunday evening, the girls only want to know one thing. Did I sleep with Henri? I shouldn't be surprised, but the idea never even crossed my mind. Henri's good looking enough, I guess. He has symmetrical features and kind eyes, but I'm just not attracted to him. His illness saps him of sex appeal. Even if we're way too young to have children, the thought of a defect in the gene pool of my hypothetical offspring quells any erotic thoughts I may have otherwise had. Scientists have observed the same instinct in rats. Females refuse to mate with sick males. As a result, sick males will do everything in their power to conceal little sores so they appear to offer top-quality genetic material. This eugenic explanation probably wouldn't go over well at school, so I just shrug my shoulders and vaguely say that he's "not my type."

I'm also at a loss to explain my obsession with the way Henri puts sunscreen on his face, a practiced movement he has clearly carried out thousands of times. He starts in the middle of his forehead and applies small dabs of cream clockwise. It's vaguely reminiscent of the face painting of Aboriginal Australians. Next he spreads it over every millimetre of his skin, including his ears.

We played video games. Henri has tons of games, on every different console. We also took long walks in the evening and talked a lot. And ate and slept a lot. And did my homework, which, given Henri's intellectual prowess, was a sorry joke.

Henri is incredibly advanced, compared to me. He's started programming computers, while we're still learning to hunt and peck on the keyboard. And he's using the internet for more than just watching the porn and gore videos that my cousins introduced to me. I didn't have the guts to show Henri the video of this old Japanese woman who throws up, eats her vomit, and then throws up again, for minutes on end. (Our game when we watched was to see who could hold out longest without throwing up themselves.) I also skipped the video of the twins, around our age, who made a porn movie in what appears to be a mobile home in the Midwest. The internet sure is full of people doing filthy things on camera!

I did make Henri watch one example of what I was talking about. Then our conversation took a turn. How much money would it take for us to agree to give a bottle of champagne a vigorous shake, pop the cork, and then shove it up our ass? Henri said ten million. On film? No, never on film, but he would rise to the challenge for a place in a bunker when the end of the world comes. I would have expected him to offer up his dignity in exchange for a body with the ability to regenerate its tissue, but that was before I knew him well enough to understand that Henri is a committed realist.

4 Bacchanalia

THE BEST day of his life came when a massive sea creature sunk into the abyss. The shark knew it would be big. Its effluvium wasn't especially strong, but it was everywhere. The water was saturated with it. The shark first circled for hours, in search of the exact source of the smell, and only later swooped down. He swam around a long time before reaching the body. He wasn't the first creature on the scene. As he drew nearer the target, he sensed other scavengers gorging themselves. But it wasn't too late. There was still plenty of food to go around. The smells, the richness of the flesh, the electrical impulses emitted by other predators: a feeding frenzy was under way. Never had he been so aware of his own body, of the strength of his jaw, the pleasure of rolling over onto himself and ripping off chunks of tallow as big as his head — a rare and bounteous meal he would spend months digesting while pursuing a large female. Life was perfect.

His thumbnail is long and thick, marbled yellow and brown. Judging by the reaction of his fellow crew members, who clap their hands and loudly laugh and sing, this man has a gift. The firelight distorts their faces. The musician plucks the strings of his instrument with his grotesque nail.

The thought of this man touching her makes Désirée flinch with disgust. The music is high-pitched and hazy. Drinking songs. She watches them from a distance. When these men come, they bring strange, deadly troubles with them. And sometimes, two seasons later, they leave lighter-skinned children behind.

The ship sailed into the bay five days ago, carrying the reek of carrion waiting to be flensed. If the odour weren't enough, the squawking of thousands of birds would have alerted the coast-dwellers.

They weren't the first whalers to drop anchor here, but they were certainly the most inept. They were looking for large ovens to render the fat, but they'd been misinformed: the ovens were several day's sail westward. The carcasses were beyond saving anyway. Such a waste!

Torn sails and missing rowboats, rotten teeth and broken limbs: the crew is in a bad way. Worst of all, they're out of fresh water. There's no knowing exactly what happened, given the language barrier. Most likely a storm, compounded by their thorough incompetence. The captain is sickly pale. He's a man of few words.

The sailors are given the usual welcome. Many ignore less-than-subtle requests to scrub off a layer of grease; all eat and drink like starved ogres. They are surprised to be served marrow on fresh-baked bread. The youngest savours his beans and lard, baked overnight with a hare in a pot buried in sand and the coals. Clearly, these men haven't enjoyed such delicacies in ages. But once the summer camp is set up, there is time to cook.

Désirée eyes the young man whose head seems to have fused with his cap. His hair is the same colour as the wool. He's not tall, but he stands up straight and smiles a lot. Unlike the others, he still has almost all his teeth. It's one of the benefits of youth. He's young enough to be her son. But no one could be her son, or her daughter for that matter. Désirée has never had children.

Something is broken inside her. She doesn't know what. She feels no pain. She looks no different than the other women. Yet her belly stays empty, and not for want of trying. Every time she feels desire for a man, she can't help but imagine what their children would look like. If she were normal inside, she'd have had a whole litter by now. Sometimes she dreams of a tiny hand resting on hers or the weight of a child sleeping on her shoulder. Her phantom pains ease as the sun rises. Désirée's life is now given over to pleasure: her own and that of the men who want her.

She always pitches her tent in the camp's outer reaches. Her presence is tolerated, but only so long as she makes herself scarce. It smarts not to be invited to the campfire with the others. She lights her own fire, sits down, and listens to the snatches of conversation and the laughter from afar. They find her infertility discomfiting. She catches a whiff of pity in the furtive looks they cast her way, and the whispers of young superstitious women who fear that her condition, like some contagious disease, might leap up and afflict them. Désirée maintains a polite distance, keeps a low profile. Her presence reminds them of hard truths no one wants to face. Some people get no luck whatsoever. Life is mostly hard. Happiness is a matter of random chance.

After all, she says, it's for the best. She wouldn't want to be in the centre of the camp, amid the cooking smells and children's shrieks and barking of dogs. Her own hound is smart and silent. Sometimes he gets mistaken for a coyote. He is fast-running, slender, and agile as a fox.

When she was little, she believed animals could take on human form. The metamorphoses occurred at night, in the inhabited heart of the forest. The therians would trade stories about ordinary humans, reflections on the tedious lives of creatures unable to shift shapes. She had yearned to walk into a clearing one night and observe these creatures. The moment she stumbled upon the thin puppy, standing still with eyes shining in a rambunctious litter of brothers and sisters, her childhood came flashing back. Désirée and the puppy adopted each other.

Désirée's French name was probably chosen by her parents to please the priest. She hasn't seen a priest for so long now, not since she joined the group of families migrating to the north-east. They moved to find a peaceful life, to get away from being told everything they did was wrong, each and every day, from morning to night. The clergy hold a static and unyielding vision of the order of things. The ones most likely to humiliate her publicly are the very same ones who would turn up at her house, trembling with excitement, and grow livid when she spurned them. It was exhausting and dangerous. An unattached, literate woman was something to be feared. Now here she is, in this land of stunted spruce and icy water. Life is hard here as well, but at least Désirée sleeps easy.

The young man with the cap looks at her often. Even tonight, with his features softened by alcohol, his gaze finds her. She sits on the promontory overlooking the rocky beach, where the sailors have gathered around a fire. He nods his head without lowering his eyes. She mirrors his movement, with no clear sense of what she is agreeing to.

Tomorrow they'll weigh anchor. Désirée has already seen them filling barrels with fresh water. They'll travel up the seaway to Tadoussac, or maybe as far as Quebec, where they'll find everything they need to repair their ship and get back on the high seas.

She suspects the captain has other plans. She knows how their world works. It all comes down to money. People whose floors crack under the weight of their provisions will walk right by starving children in the street. These sailors may be penniless, but the captains sometimes have something laid by. The ship owners pay them handsomely. She's heard of sailors leaving behind wives and children to cross the ocean, take possession of lands, start new lives on foreign shores. Some simply disappear into the wilderness.

The ship sets sail the next day, leaving two men sleeping on the beach and the three half-decomposed carcasses. No one knows what to do with these great heaps of fat and flesh. In their advanced state of putrefaction, they aren't fit for human consumption. The locals slice off enough bait to catch hundreds of fish. The smell is truly pestilential. The abandoned sailors make crude gestures to suggest burying the massive bodies. No one wants to do it. They'll have to move camp.

An opaque white fog has risen. The dark edge of forest that rings the bay is scarcely visible. Shrill caws of crows pierce the roar of surf. The young sailor finds Désirée harvesting the mussels that have attached themselves to the kelp along the grey beach. He speaks neither French nor her language, but she now knows his name. Leo gets down on hand and knee and draws in the sand a crude map of the North Atlantic. In the Baltic Sea, Désirée sees an eagle's open wing. Denmark reminds her of a hungry baby bird. Western Europe is the scapula of some giant beast, with the fluffy ears of a bat. Leo uses stones for islands: Iceland, Newfoundland, Notiskuan. He finishes off his drawing with a seal frolicking in the great waters of the river, along the path that led Leo there.

Désirée can't tear her eyes from his mangled hands. His palms are covered in callouses. His knuckles have been split by the salt water. Scabs in various stages of healing run down to his elbows. White and pink scars striate his forearms and the back of his hands. She can sense the splinters left behind by the handles of heavy oars and harpoons; hooks accidentally planted; sharp, heavy nets hoisted aboard; ropes grasped at any cost to stave off certain death. Leo points out various places on the map with his stick. He tells the story of his travels in a hodgepodge of languages Désirée doesn't know. His English is no better than hers, so they stick to sign language. They laugh a lot.

They boil the mussels she harvested in a large pot. They eat slowly. A cold rain falls over the camp, and everyone takes shelter inside. Désirée is amazed by the blond hair, soft as down, that covers the young man's body in places, and this smooth, soft skin that has been spared from his labours.

Désirée explains that she and her people are travelling inland for the winter. She does her best to describe the pristine white of snow, the bright blue sky, the taste of fatty meat; Leo would rather board a ship carrying raw logs, drift slowly toward the wars out west. Her young companion of the last few months will be leaving. He can't resist the call of the sea. Unbeknownst to him, he'll leave this place having succeeded where all others failed. Désirée will be a mother.

Low tide. The eviscerated whales lie in the clay soil under swarms of flies and flocks of birds. Dozens of bears are gathering. Some are squabbling over the choice bits; others wait their turn. A mother and her two cubs have been swimming for a long time, drawn by the smell. She's out of milk. She is famished, and so fierce that the large males retreat long enough for her and her pups to have a few sorely needed mouthfuls. Soon, their white fur is splattered with muck and black blood. These three bears set off northward, into the pink horizon. The sun has found a breach in the fog, just after setting, and its light illuminates the tops of the clouds in garish reds and purples.

The North Atlantic right whale (Eubalaena glacialis), *also known as the black whale, is so called because it was the "right" whale to hunt. It was slow, not overly fearful, and so full of blubber it would keep floating even after being killed, making it easy to tow — in all ways the ideal prey. Thanks to these qualities, the right whale was almost completely exterminated by the commercial whale hunt. To this day, it is among the most threatened whales in the world, a sad distinction shared with the blue whale. A small population survives between the Bay of Fundy and the Gulf of St. Lawrence. Though no longer hunted, these whales are often struck by ships or tangled up in fishing nets. If they avoid these risks, right whales can live up to eighty years ...*

My term paper is a slog. It's not that the subject isn't interesting. Quite the opposite — all I want to do now is watch whale movies, listen to whale sounds, read every fascinating whale article ever published. I've never done so much research for a course. I reread my paragraph, disappointed. I can't properly channel the rage flaring up inside me. For long decades we decimated these magnificent, intelligent creatures to fill our oil lamps and lubricate our machines. Now we're bombarding the survivors with our seismic probes, engines, and plastic waste.

We ram them with cargo ships laden with cheap crap. We tie them up in cables until they drown, just so we can enjoy shellfish for a few weeks every year. And that's at the best of times.

I rein myself in. After all, this is my science homework, not an environmental manifesto. The purpose of the assignment is to show that I understand the scientific classification of species. I've chosen to explore the difference between two often-confused types of right wales. The North Atlantic right whale and the bowhead whale are distinct genera of the family *Balaenidae*: baleen whales without dorsal fins or jugular furrows (Parvorder *mysticetes*, Infraroder *Cetacea*, clade Eutheria [placental], subclass *Theria*, class *Mammalia*, phylum *Chordata*, etc.)

It was the British zoologist John Edward Gray who suggested, in 1821, that the genus Balaena *is monotypic, consisting of a single species, the bowhead whale* (Balaena mysticetus). *The debate raged for 180 years before genetics finally settled the matter in the early 2000s. The genus* Eubalaena *has three species —* australis, *the above-described* glacialis, *and* japonica *— the genus* Balaena, *only one.*

Balaena mysticetus *is also known as the Greenland whale. One of its most spectacular characteristics is longevity. These mammals can live over two hundred years. In May 2005, a specimen was killed off the coast of Alaska. Lodged deep in its neck fat, they found fragments of the point of an explosive harpoon that was later identified as being manufactured around 1890 in New Bedford, Massachusetts. The animal probably survived a chase more than a century earlier before being discovered. They estimated it was 211 years old.*

At least one good thing came out of that assignment: it cemented my desire to be a marine biologist. Luckily, I'd chosen to study on the shore of the St. Lawrence. Rent is cheap, and when I open my bedroom window, I hear the sea. After spending seven years sharing dorms and apartments, living alone is more or less the lap of luxury. In my last place I had four roommates. The bathroom and kitchen were war zones.

I've been eighteen for two weeks now: officially an adult. When my dad called on the night of my birthday, it caught me by surprise. I'd lost track of the date, what with my move and my course load and my new life. I told him I was doing well, and the salt air agreed with me. He said he was happy for me and relieved. I hadn't realized he was so nervous to have me move away from home. As far as I was concerned, I'd more or less left home at eleven. He promised to come visit me when he has a few days off.

He's been appointed North American sales director for his company. That means he's the one who tells the sales force where to go and what corporate events to attend. He's had to learn to use the internet to keep up with the industry. Organic products have been cutting into the company's sales, but my father has managed to hold on to his job. He says it's thanks to my advice, but I doubt it. My dad's a lot smarter than he thinks.

I owe Henri a lot. As if by some sort of osmosis, his intellect seems to have rubbed off on me. He pushed me to take my high school exams a year earlier, just like he did. I had to do something to take advantage of all the time I'd spent watching him study, testing his memory and his comprehension of concepts. Then one day, to my surprise, there it was in the mail: my diploma. I was ready for college.

The following two years went by in the blink of an eye. My years of boarding were over. I rented an apartment near the college. There was no way I was going to keep living off my dad. I picked strawberries, raspberries, blueberries, and flowers. I even worked as a garbage woman. It would have been a lucrative gig if I hadn't broken down after three hours. I just couldn't take the stench. So I mowed lawns and planted shrubs. I installed above-ground pools. Put up fences, washed windows. I served ice cream, gasoline, coffee, quinoa salads, and cricket-flour biscuits. Study, work, chat with Henri: that about sums up my last two years. Even if I'd been old enough to go out to the bars with all the other freshly legal students, I just didn't have the time. I would have had to stop sleeping.

I bought all the required textbooks second-hand. And I'm still sleeping in my tattered old "Genuine Soft-Serve" T-shirt. The collars and hems of all the clothes I own are stained with insect repellent, which is a must when you're working outside back home. Otherwise, behind your ears will grow sticky with blood and lymph, not to mention the constant buzzing around the edge of your hair and your neck. Before long you're waking up in the middle of the night to scratch, and the next day your pillows are stained with blood. Your bites burn when you take a shower, and soon you start itching, and they start oozing again the moment you're dry.

Where I grew up, you could always tell who was new from the constellation of little sores on their neck, face, and fingers. Some people would have allergic reactions. Their ears would swell up and their eyes would get all puffy, if the insects got up that high. The stupidest people would hold out for three weeks, and when they finally decided to apply a real DDT-based mosquito repellent, their wounds would sting horribly. Did I mention the repellent probably causes cancer too?

But here in Rimouski, on the St. Lawrence Seaway, blood-sucking insects don't seem to be a problem. It must be the wind. After my conversation with my father, I take a look around my apartment — the naked bulb on my ceiling, the yellowed walls, the white melamine cupboards, the beige appliances, the table covered in whitish stains. A cardboard box labelled "Random — kitchen" in black marker is still resting on the counter. Aside from the chair I was sitting on (too low), my living room contained nothing but a little brown ottoman and a square blue fifteen-dollar coffee table from Ikea. In the bedroom, my mattress lay on the floor. My clothes were carefully rolled on a set of metal shelves I'd found by the side of the road the day I got here. I had three plates, a few mismatched cereal bowls, and two mugs bearing the logo of my father's company — SSE, Sanitation Solutions Experts.

I decided to buy myself a brand-new computer for my birthday. It was the first one I'd ever had just for me. When I wasn't able to use Henri's, I was usually the only person writing up assignments in my college computer lab. Most of the other students only came to the lab to play online games, driving me crazy with their frantic clicking. Others would program little scripts to get around paywalls and watch free porn. I vowed I would never deal with sticky keyboards again!

Thanks to a scholarship, I'll be able to focus exclusively on my studies for my first year of university. With a little luck, I'll spend next summer counting larvae in the middle of a pond, instead of dealing with insufferable customers complaining that their coffee is too cold or too hot or too warm.

As for Henri, he's still living in the basement of the same grey house, three hundred metres from my high school. He's coding the program that will manage a telescope studying the sun. He claims it's easy work. The engineers provide the co-ordinates. He doesn't actually calculate anything, just carefully enters the data in the program he designed. The orbiting telescope rotates itself, focuses its own lens, and sends the high-resolution photos it takes back to earth. This makes Henri one of the few people on earth who have intimate access to the sun.

He talks about emigrating to the States to work for NASA full time. His current gig pays so well that his mom quit her job. More than once, he's offered to pay for stuff for me — tuition, rent, groceries. But I'm not having it. I know he thinks I'm working too much, and it's cutting into our time to hang out. He still can't go outside without his spaceman suit. He wishes I could live underground with him, and we could go out at night, like those cute little bug-eyed lemurs. He didn't call on my birthday. He's still sulking because I left town.

* * *

It's wild how much free time I have now that I don't have to work to pay tuition. I'm ahead on all my term projects. (I got an A+ on my term paper on right whales, thanks for asking.) And I landed an internship with my favourite instructor next summer. We're going to measure oxygen concentrations and the presence of certain plankton species at different various depths in the St. Lawrence River. To break the good news, my instructor smiled and asked if I got seasick.

It was a very cold winter. I'd read that the weather is milder near large bodies of water. Well, I call bullshit! Out here on the St. Lawrence, the humidity chills you to the bone and the wind never lets up.

Finally, we get a nice spring day, sun that does more than just diffuse a cold light. To explore the woods behind the campus, I borrow a pair of snowshoes from a classmate who worked with me on an assignment about the nervous system of the octopus.

It's really early and it's Saturday, so most people are still sleeping. The forest is all mine. We've had a lot of snow these last few weeks, and the snowshoes sink into the powder without a sound. I can see the tracks of hares, and different kinds of birds — maybe partridges? I've been walking for an hour or so when I emerge into a small clearing. I decide to take a break. I pull out my Thermos and pour myself a cup of coffee.

After a few sips, I notice that the atmosphere has changed. The sky has clouded over, the birds have stopped chirping. The only sound is the wind whistling through the evergreens swaying all around me. And that's when I see it, high up in an ash tree, just a few metres away. The twin yellow eyes of a great horned owl are looking right at me. We stare each other down for several minutes. Then, without a sound, it spreads its large brown wings and flies away. It circles the clearing a few times, then disappears toward the west. A great sadness comes over me. My father has come to see me, to say goodbye.

His funeral is the following week, just before exams. It's an intimate gathering. My aunt Élie is there, with my uncle Réjean and my cousins William, Laurent, and Kevin. Yannick couldn't make it: he and his girlfriend had twins a few weeks ago. They live in Ontario.

There are also three people from my father's work, including one woman who cries a lot and someone from the church. Does he even count? I don't know. He was recommended by the person responsible for my father's burial at the funeral home. All I had to do was sign a few papers. My dad had paid for everything in advance. The obituary had been drafted for the newspaper and the website. Even after everyone was named in full, it wasn't very long.

My father had chosen a place for his urn in the columbarium where Pachelbel's *Canon* plays on eternal repeat. I would have expected him to want to be buried, like my mother, but no. Their remains aren't even in the same town.

Another difference from my mother's burial is that the sky is a brilliant blue. I drove out to the funeral in a Yaris I borrowed from a classmate who plans to devote his career to studying how plants communicate through their root systems. Eight hours there today; eight hours back tomorrow. I'll stay the night at Aunt Élie's, just like the good old days. My cousins and I settle in the basement. My aunt reopened her daycare a few years ago. The room has filled back up with toys of every colour.

I stay up late with Laurent and Kevin. William and his parents are sleeping upstairs. After a few beers and a couple joints, Kevin brings out the heavy artillery. The white powder gleams on the tiny doll mirror. I'm stationed at the woodworking shop; Laurent is seated at Paw Patrol headquarters. Kevin has put on a long green wig from the costume box. I wish I could do something concrete to mark my father's death. Take a shovel and patiently dig him a grave, until I could feel the pain in my arms and the sweat on my brow and get blisters on my fingers. Instead, I'm a useless bystander in this process, armed with a ballpoint pen and a dressy blouse I bought in a hurry on my way through Quebec City. It was a shock to be handed the urn with his ashes to place on the shelf in the columbarium. It was so light.

In my aunt and uncle's basement, I'm having fun with playdough. I try to sculpt a realistic replica of my father's heart. Which, they told me, had failed. A partially obstructed valve. His heart swelled up. At the end it was twice the size of a normal organ. There wasn't enough playdough to finish my piece. Only when Laurent takes me in his arms do I realize I'm crying.

I get sick several times on the drive home. I have to pull over onto the shoulder to open the door and lean out, with my hair in my eyes, waiting for the nausea to pass. Portly retirees in worn leather pass by on their three-wheeled motorcycles. They slow down but don't change lanes, eyeing me with an air of disapproval. "The fuck you want?" I yell out at one. "Get lost!"

The rush of adrenalin that comes after this feat of boldness pushes me back onto my feet. I realize I could just keep driving, in a straight line, in any direction of my choosing — north or south, anywhere or nowhere — and not one single person would care. Obviously, my classmate would like me to return his "ride," as he likes to call it. But I still get the feeling that at this very moment I could disappear from the face of the earth and it wouldn't cross anyone's mind to go looking for me. I'm an orphan now.

5 Sprezzatura

DESPAIR IS setting in. Though the whales have been swimming for hours, the water is disturbingly clear. They are spread evenly throughout the area, a few hundred metres apart. Normally they stay close, but this situation calls for desperate measures. Periodically they call out their positions, to keep safe and make sure no corner of the water is forgotten. A few have found small, rich pockets of marine life, but there aren't enough to feed the whole pod. After a few mouthfuls, nothing would remain for the others. Normally at this time of year, the food is so plentiful you can barely see your own tail.

The old whale is weakening. She makes multiple attempts to move out into the open waters, to let herself sink down in peace, away from her predators and out of reach of her community. They block her way. The old whale lacks energy for this final confrontation. She stops and waits for what is coming. She can sense the alarm in the faces of the nieces and great-nieces responsible for her escort. Their Oracle is precious, irreplaceable. Countless times her songs have made their way through these waters. They come to hear her and also to confide in her, to tell her their own stories. Oracle is all-knowing, all-seeing, all-understanding. But at this moment, the matriarch wants only to fully clear her mind and die.

She thinks of her descendants. She has only given birth to males, who all left her just weeks after weaning.

What a joy to see those chubby, fearful little creatures grow into playful, adventurous adolescents. The cousins formed a little gang. Later they would set off to conquer new territories, seek out unknown females to seduce. The boldest among them would lunge right into the pack ice, making it crack even where it lay thickest. Wounds acquired this way stand as symbols of their strength. The weaker, softer-headed ones sometimes drowned, it's true.

Of the many children she bore over her long life, she has only seen three again after they left. The first she encountered short hours after he proudly left the group of his relatives. Floating with his tongue ripped out by killer whales, as sharks gnawed away at the thick fat whose growth she had so carefully monitored every day for the past year. Her maternal instincts kicked in and she lashed out at the dead body and the sharks and everything else around them. Bellowing could be heard for kilometres all around her. After a while, relatives she hadn't seen for years found her there, defending the cadaver in vain. She has no memory of the months that followed.

A harpoon came to an abrupt halt in the second one's skull. She hadn't seen him in sixty years when, through an unfortunate turn of events, she recognized his distress call: a sequence of low-frequency sounds whose rhythm hadn't changed since childhood. Following her instinct, she sought out its source, ignoring the voice of fear ordering her to flee in the opposite direction.

The water ran red. Though she had escaped many a bloody hunt, she had never seen so much blood, so many dead whales in a single spot. Two of her nephews also fell victim. The factory ship slowly hoisted the carcasses into its hull. For lack of space, the whalers left behind almost half the day's kill. Someone had been trigger-happy on the harpoon gun.

She met the third of her calves much farther south, when it again became possible to venture out without risking impalement. They had often seen each other over the last few decades, when she used to swim along the coastline to the point where the water became too warm to bear. He was leaner than she was, and faster too. A handsome creature, with very few scars: unlike his relatives further north, he hadn't grown up with the constant need to break through the ice. Then, one night she felt a pang of joy on recognizing his song in the middle of the bay. She saw a much scrawnier creature. He was struggling to swim, unable to shake off the long filaments trailing in his wake. Unable to dive, he was certain to perish. Without turning around, she left behind the bountiful, noisy bay to begin her northward migration alone.

Humans have devised filaments thin enough to capture even the smallest marine creatures. Maybe it was jealousy of her species' superior jaws that drove them to destroy so many of her kind. They built a giant facsimile, ringed with the baleens pulled from their victims' jaws to filter the water, leaving no living creature behind. That must be why they stopped hunting: they've gathered enough baleens to empty the entire ocean. She fears this terrifying apparatus that swallows everything in its path, leaving behind only clear, lifeless water.

As she draws on her last reserves of strength, the whale hears the young females holding a conclave. Even if they find a hypothetical pocket of krill, the venerable elder may not be able to feed with them. They can't regurgitate food into her mouth, as seagulls feed their young. After a time, the fattest among them, one of the few to calve this year, swims slowly toward Oracle. Its calf works hard to breathe on its own. The old whale has often looked after it when its mother sets off in search of food. It is tiny. It drinks little, chokes often.

The female stretches out her belly in Oracle's direction. Though the old whale hasn't suckled for two centuries, her tongue recalls the twist that forms a tube to her throat. It's a strange, comforting feeling. She is surprised by the milk's warmth and unctuous richness. She drinks ravenously and at length. A second young mother relieves the first. The matriarch has a great appetite. When she has finally slaked her thirst and come back to her senses, she starts singing with all her might. Her song is a call to leave behind this horrible, sterile place. It is time to move on. The covering of pack ice is thick — too thick in places — but instinct tells her she can break through. What are a few more scars? Better than letting herself die. They will pierce through the eternal ice cap, summon forth a new ocean, if that's what it takes.

Though the kitchen is stifling, the windows stay shut. The greenish light that filters in casts a gloomy pall over the room. She has lit a few candles to better see the contents of the cauldron. You can't produce remedies for thirty years undisturbed without taking certain precautions.

First and foremost: complete discretion. Every time she "cooks," Simone burns cabbage leaves to mask the exotic scents that have suffused the kitchen. Only after these occult aromas have been neutralized does she permit herself to open windows and doors. The neighbourhood laughs at her. Rumour has it she's a terrible cook; people pity her son. Some gossips go so far as to say it's her lack of skill in the kitchen that made him "that way." Yet Simone can roast meat and potatoes and bake bread. Her son gets fed just like all the other boys.

The water has been boiling a few minutes. She adds sugar, ginger, red peppers, and hemp flowers — instead of the absinthe that proved to have more dangerous side effects. This decision came after the episode with the notary during her stay in France. He was found buck naked on the roof of his house, yelling for all to hear that he had found the cloud where God was hiding. She'd very clearly instructed his wife to administer exactly seven sips — no more, no less. The wife clearly hadn't heeded the instructions. Simone had had to flee before dawn. She spent a few weeks hiding out in the mountains. Once her paranoia subsided, she booked passage on the next ship for North America. It was time to go home. She was pregnant, to boot.

She pulls the cauldron off the fire, mixes in tea leaves, a single tiny button of peyote (no more!), dried mushrooms, and cocoa powder. Once the mixture has cooled a little, she filters it and adds ten drops of human blood. Meaning hers. It's all she has. She tastes the concoction. It's ready.

She spots an ant crawling on the wooden counter, drawn by the sugar crystals that have dropped from the spoon. She watches it wriggle its antennae and quickly but gently picks it up between her thumb and forefinger. On a cruel whim, she crushes it and adds it to her broth. Will the ants realize that their scout never made it back?

She pours the fragrant brown broth into a liquor bottle she has painstakingly cleaned, then lays the concoction under the turnips in the root cellar of her wooden house in the heart of the village. She scrubs everything clean and stores her precious ingredients, with labels decipherable to her alone, in their small metal chest. She's not about to let herself meet the same fate as La Corriveau: hanged and left out by the roadside for all to see. It had been her grandmother's favourite story, the one she always told when she was feeling mean. It's an exemplar of human barbarism, and a morality tale on the need to keep your difference hidden away at all costs. She never failed to deliver the moral of the story — "Everything's allowed, so long as you don't get caught!" — and then she'd burst out laughing, exposing the few decaying stumps of teeth left in her ravaged mouth. What little hair she had left was tied up in a small blackish bun. She liked to claim that she only had seven white hairs, but then the truth, for Didi, had always been an elastic concept. Her black pupils would shine, almost entirely covered by her droopy eyelids. She may have been shrivelled up like a prune, but still she moved with an astonishing agility.

Didi loved telling stories of what a great sailor Simone's grandfather had been. He wasn't born on land, the legend had it, but emerged from the water on the back of a whale. About her grandfather, there were only two things Simone knew for sure. One, he was white. Two, he left and never came back.

"Good riddance" was all her grandmother said. What would she have done anyway, with a man forever getting in her way? She had her daughter, and of course she had her grandchildren. She loved nothing better than stuffing them with sweets until they threw up, then terrorizing them with stories. Didi kept telling Simone about the mysteries of the forest, the medicinal plants, and surprising animal behaviour. At first, Simone thought these were tall tales. She figured her grandmother was touched in the head. But over the years she came to see that nearly everything her grandmother had told her was true. Except of course her grandfather's origin story.

Simone fingers the small packet of bones she keeps in a velvet pouch at the very bottom of the chest. The pinkie of her grandmother's left hand. She would have preferred a skull, but she was thousands of miles away when Didi died. Her brothers had gone and chosen the finger the old lady had always used to clean their ears. Simone figured a long time must have passed since their ear canals got a thorough scraping. She pitied her brothers' wives. But then rubbing up against someone's dirty ear must be better than kissing a sour-tasting mouth. But then maybe the wives were as filthy as their husbands.

Her brothers claimed to be practical people. They opted for the relic that would be easiest to preserve. All Simone has to do is dig up the cadaver and boil its head, if she's so attached to it. She sends them to the devil and contents herself with the little finger.

The older she gets, the more she thinks about her grandmother. What would she have said about her son, Paul? Simone prides herself on her ability to read people's intentions at a glance, but her son is a closed book.

If he were a prospective customer, she'd deny everything. Denying that she has anything for sale is her go-to strategy with new clients anyway. She claims to have savings, dating back to her years in Europe. Suggests that a combination of frugal lifestyle and Christian charity save her from stooping to the acts she is rumoured to commit.

She serves her clients a drink, lets their confidences unspool. Only those deemed to be in genuine need will be served. The thrill-seekers and busybodies see her as no more than a second-rate artist, a penniless hawker with no real talent, a victim of gossip.

With those who pass the test, those she decides she can trust, she claims to be long out of the business, but willing to make an exception. As they'll be the only ones in the community aware of her gifts, she'll know who it was right away if word gets out. She ends her speech with a short initiation ceremony designed to quash the germ of any future betrayal. It's a simple but highly effective ritual designed to scare them — no more. She carefully closes the doors. She draws the curtains. Lights a black candle. Burns some juniper seeds, says a few words in Latin (a passage from the Book of Revelation does nicely). Then she places her palm on her client's palm and spits on them. That's all. Full payment in advance. She'll deliver the goods when the time is right. And don't bother asking how it's coming along. When it's ready, Simone will find you.

The love potion is Simone's most lucrative and least effective elixir. That isn't to say it's entirely useless. It's more that its effect has little to do with amorous desire. It's an invigorating tonic that instills a sense of euphoria, especially when taken on an empty stomach. Just enough to spark a fire, as Didi would say.

She always gives detailed advice on how to get the best results. Drink exactly seven sips of the mixture. The person you desire must do the same, but remain unaware of the nature of the potion. Provided the dosage is respected, it's acceptable to dilute it in another liquid, to mask its taste. You must then spend at least three hours in the company of the beloved. Exchange at least ten sentences; prepare their favourite foods. If you follow all these guidelines and love still eludes you, you can kiss this relationship goodbye. What Simone doesn't let on is that her potion is merely accessory to these rites of seduction. Drinking the tonic makes you feel elated. With a little luck, this feeling of well-being will be ascribed to the budding romance.

The recipe is simple; procuring ingredients is more challenging. You can substitute black pepper for the hot peppers, but the result is far less appetizing. She has built a small glass hothouse, barely larger than the dresser, for plants intolerant of northern climates. She grows more common plants there as well and gives seedlings out to the villagers who keep vegetable gardens. She has two: the classic garden next to her house and a second one that she tends with a care bordering on obsession in a clearing near the stream behind the church. The chances of the fat, rheumatic priest exploring every inch of his domain are slim. If he did, he probably wouldn't notice the exotic plants that stick out in this landscape like sore thumbs. And even if he had the botanical knowledge to understand what made the plants all around so unusual, he'd probably be content to praise the mystery of God's work.

Simone was at first hesitant to use blood, from any source. She thought it was superfluous, devoid of properties that would improve her potions' taste or enhance their effect. Also, unless you keep farm animals, fresh blood is hard to come by. It was a lot of hassle just to add a macabre touch and fill out the body of a recipe otherwise not much different from the tonics sold by apothecaries and wandering peddlers. But in practice, each time the potion worked, her own blood had been added. Since there's little margin of error in her line of work, she made it a regular ingredient.

The first time she cut her forehead, right near the hairline, torrential rains poured down on her cabin. Simone can recognize a sign when she sees one. Now it rains every time she prepares a potion, without fail. The blood must be fresh and must drip straight from her wound into the potion. This last rule is nowhere made explicit, but Simone has learned to follow her intuition.

Recently she's been wondering whether her dark art is bringing her misfortune. She watches her blood flow, feels that she might be witnessing her very essence diluting into the vast world. Colours fade, food loses its taste. Even the sight of her son, which once filled her with joy, now leaves her indifferent. There he is walking back from school, soaked by the storm that took the whole village by surprise.

He's a handsome boy. Everyone has always said so. Even now, as a teenager, there's a purity about him that tugs at your heartstrings when you linger over his cherubic features. His pale skin, green eyes, and curly brown hair; the perfect symmetry of his lips, nose, and brow. He's admired everywhere he goes, like a purebred. If she hadn't carried him inside her for nine months and pushed him out into the world in such excruciating pain, she would struggle to believe this gorgeous creature is really her son. His father had a moustache and powerful forearms. Not exactly handsome, but undeniably attractive. She can no longer remember his face.

The boy puts on dry clothes and silently hands over his soaked shirt and pants. The rain has washed away the dust. His knuckles hurt. They've turned red, but the skin hasn't cracked. The other guy must still be down on the ground, in the undergrowth, trying to catch his breath. Paul could have kept pummelling him until all breathing stopped, but he's no killer. He doesn't know how much time he has until his opponent tells the others and the whole village cries out for vengeance. A few hours, tops. He'll have dinner with Simone, give her a hug, wait until she falls asleep. Watch her attentively and with a heavy heart. After that, he'll never see his mother again.

Like everyone else in the world, I'm watching the Mars launch live. Thirty of us employees have assembled in the conference room. Alexander tossed five boxes of Twinkies into the centre of the table. I'm on my fourth wagon wheel. And then there's Birthe, who spent the previous evening cutting up veggies. Her carrot and celery sticks wait patiently on their plate. Only a few slices of bell pepper have found takers. Philippe has taken out his cigars, and I hope the sprinkler system won't detect a threat to our physical safety. If I were him, I'd have waited for at least a successful landing. Or better yet, the end of the expedition.

I mean, the rest of us are making do with mugs of lukewarm coffee laced with a little cannabis oil. We've closed the blinds to block out the white winter light. Our eyes are glued to the 360-degree projection of Cape Canaveral. The archival footage will be much sharper than the Apollo 11 moon landing. Future generations will even be able to experience this in extreme-sensory reality.

There's an hour to go until the final countdown, but there's also no way anything productive is going to happen this afternoon. We've fed all our little creatures. The tanks have been powered down, the lights dimmed. The smartest creatures in the aquarium aren't fooled, but it's not like the fish are going to rise up and rebel.

The live feed commentators are waxing lyrical about the Quebec engineers' invaluable contribution to the Mars adventure. They developed an auxiliary device for calibrating the atmosphere on the ship in the event that the main system fails. I wouldn't go so far as to say that we collectively want this to happen. But it *would* be the only way to prove our expertise.

The Mars mission has monopolized the news for weeks now. It was high time for an event the whole world could get behind, since the networks had wrung everything they could from the story of the rabid raccoons. Try as they might to prohibit tourists from feeding the raccoons that live on Mount Royal, it wasn't long before the guides got to know the schedule of the police responsible for enforcing the law there. The moment the peace officers get back on their horses to make their rounds of the trails, the tourists take out their kibble. Most have never seen wild animals in their natural habitat, and they are willing to pay dearly for the privilege of sharing this experience with their children. The guides claim the rabies story was made up to mess with their business. The live news channels have squeezed every last drop of juice out of this rumour. No one has managed to capture an animal that was actually foaming at the mouth. So the Mars Mission came just in time.

The population is struggling to remember the names of the martyrs for science who will be taking part in the mission. It doesn't help that none of them exactly look like Matt Damon. What *has* caught hold of the popular imagination is the scatological science that made this space travel possible. The astronauts' urine will be recycled countless times, significantly reducing the amount of drinking water that must be brought along. And their feces will be used in two ways. Once the water has been filtered out, it will serve as fertilizer for edible plants that generate oxygen. More impressively, it will also be burned as rocket fuel for the return journey. Conventional fuel is heavy and unstable. This ingenious solution to the problem has made headlines around the world.

I can never remember the real name of the mission. Around here we call it the POO Rocket. Thousands of memes are going around on social media. NASA engineers say the hardest person to convince of this promising alternative fuel source was the president of the United States. He didn't want to look ridiculous. Too bad, sucker. God, I love science!

Everything has been thought out down to the last detail, but there's still so much that could go wrong. Henri and I have talked about this a lot. He had the perfect psychological profile to join the Mars mission. One, he's used to living in a vacuum, and two, he's unflappable. Physically, it's a different story though. While it's true that his digestive system produces very little flatulence, which I personally consider a key requirement for this type of mission, his body's inability to repair cells whose DNA has been damaged makes him unfit for space travel.

Travelling to Mars in a tin can exposes you to huge amounts of solar radiation, levels far greater than what reaches us on the surface of the earth. Without the combined protection of the atmosphere and a magnetic field, the human body is essentially immersed in an X-ray machine for two years. Yes, that's the preposterous length of the mission. Seven months to get to Mars, seven months to come home, and ten months on Mars to conduct experiments, set up a human camp, and produce enough fuel — we all know what *that* means — for the return journey.

Henri has resigned himself to not personally making the trip, but he's still putting his programming talents to work for the mission. I've always known he was a genius. I'm just glad to see the rest of humanity finally taking notice.

Henri now lives in the NASA complex in Florida: the Sunshine State. If he weren't such a committed rationalist, I might imagine that his choice of location was a cynical joke. I used to joke around with him that he could at least abuse his power a little by allocating a tiny portion of his budget — say 0.0001 percent — to fund my modest research projects. But I have to admit, he went one better. In his spare time, he bootstrapped together a custom-made program for my coral. Water temperature and salinity, oxygen level, light duration and intensity — even ocean currents can be reproduced in my aquarium. I just enter the numbers in the console and … bingo! With a simple request, I can start the spawning period for hundreds of fish species. No more waiting for the hypothetical full moon that comes once every three years. It's simple enough that a monkey could take over my computer with the same results.

My doctoral research involved reproducing the living conditions of a coral reef in Belize. I secretly hoped that the government would bankroll a Caribbean vacation for me, but in the entire three years I spent on the project, I only got to spend a few days in the tropics: just long enough to collect my samples. All the data about their living conditions had already been compiled. My goal was to reproduce them in vitro. What difference did it make if the temperature outside the lab was minus twenty-seven degrees Celsius?

Clearing customs on my return trip was the most thrilling moment in my life. If I hadn't told a few strategic lies, I'd still be waiting to get out of there. I claimed I was bringing back samples of seventeen different species. In fact, I had microscopic quantities of over three thousand, tucked away in five high-tech coolers on loan from the university. That's a lot of eggs. Because I had to focus on species that would travel well, my bags were free of whale sharks. I identified each sample by number, so there would be no way of knowing what it was unless you had either my master list or a microscope handy.

I had all the required environmental approvals for the few species I did declare, but I still had to wait nearly four hours at Canadian customs while they went through the bags of water hooked up to the microcomputers in their coolers. Luckily the customs officials didn't dig too deeply.

It's not like I was supplying some illegal smuggling network for endangered aquatic species. I was actually doing the very opposite of poaching: my aim was to save these species. My veneer of keen grad-student and a smattering of scientific jargon saved the day. It was a relief when I could finally leave the airport with my precious cargo. They let me out in the nick of time: the cooler batteries were running out of juice. I was able to charge them in the shuttle sent specially to pick me up, but we still had to stop once an hour at charging stations to keep the vehicle powered up enough to make it to the university.

Eighty percent of my microscopic passengers survived the voyage. Starting more or less from scratch, I raised each species, individually or in small groups, as I waited to collect enough biomass to provide a habitat where these creatures could live together as one big happy family.

There were aquariums all over — in my labs, in classrooms, in my apartment, at my friends' and colleagues' and professors' places. I was using a sophisticated aquarium-management system that you can buy in pet shops. It had LED lighting, a pump, and temperature and salinity regulators. Henri hacked the application it came with so we could regulate other variables as well. Soon I was managing dozens of ecosystems from my smartphone. I'd get an alert whenever something wasn't right. Needless to say, I didn't get much sleep in those three years.

We were able to successfully recreate the breeding conditions of coral and the fish. My dissertation is essentially a step-by-step guide you could follow to create your very own coral reef at home. Three months after I submitted it, the committee in charge of setting up the aquarium division of the Saint-Félicien Nature Park (known as the Saint-Félicien Zoo, until the communications team decided to scratch the word *zoo* from all promotional material) contacted me to implement a large-scale reproduction program for the main marine ecosystems.

When I joined the team, there were five of us crammed into an office much smaller than my student apartment. The government had given us a grant, and there was still so much left to be done: present specifications, get the necessary approvals, build the facilities, import the large specimens, attract tourists, and the list went on.

To say I'm proud of what we accomplished is a massive understatement. Today there's only one place left in the world where you can admire a coral reef in all its splendour, and that's through the large window of the Saint-Félicien Nature Park. The artificial water reservoir is home to 2,481 species. Most are microscopic but nonetheless essential. The plankton is so dense in places that it makes the water cloudy. Multicoloured coral has proliferated into veritable cities, filtering this festive mess with their colonies of active bacteria.

Fish of all shapes and sizes, hatched from the eggs I brought in, swim along in tight schools, while others hunt alone. We give them enough fish food to survive, but most of their calories come from whatever they hunt or scavenge. A lot of new fish have been introduced over the years as well, which both enriches and complicates my work. I'm happy I was able to save my living collection. But recreating an entire world from scratch sure takes a lot of energy. Everyone close to me was getting more than a little tired of all the miniature floods and the ammoniac scent of the tanks.

The aquarium is now part of Project GIZMO (Grand International Zoos Main Objective, named, of course, after the adorable gremlin). It's an international network of artificial ecosystems, a contemporary Noah's Ark designed to save endangered species.

The white rhinoceros, the orangutan, the vaquita, the chorus frog, and the myriad other marine creatures no longer found in nature — all have survived because they are attractive to tourists. While we tried to figure out where to house the very ugliest species, we had frozen their gametes.

The pessimists believe it's now too late. The tropical oceans teem with poisonous jellyfish and lionfish scavenging in chalky beds of dead coral. In rivers thick with slimy algae, you can still catch obese carp, but not much else. Too bad they taste like mud. Not even dogs will eat them. They get ground up into pellets for fish farms. Then the droppings of these fish fertilize the algae, completing the lifecycle. To say we've given up is an understatement. These are dark times. I'm reminded of the slogan of the Mars mission: *We Hope*.

Célestin wants to have a talk. I guess she's technically my boss, but I think of her more as a friend. She has a gift for seeing the big picture. Unlike me, when she decides to do something, she knows exactly what she's getting herself into. The floor-to-ceiling bookshelves in her office are overflowing with books, file folders, and scientific journals. Papers form piles on the floor and on her worktable. Her computer keyboard rests precariously on a stack of binders bursting with scholarly journals and handwritten notes.

In the centre of this glorious disarray, Célestin reigns supreme. She's more confident than I am in a dress, gorgeous with her stout, hairy forearms shimmering under the lab's fluorescent lights. You have to admire her style. Her employees nicknamed her "Tintin" seventeen years ago, because the last syllable rhymes with her given name, and it stuck.

Before she lowers the blind, I notice that it's started snowing. Once we're in partial darkness, it gets easier to see the images projected on the screen in the middle of the room. There's a map of the Arctic, a research vessel, and a list of species written out in Latin, English, and French. I see the names of our scientist colleagues, which seem vaguely familiar. They must have written articles I've read.

Tintin starts in abruptly on the subject of the Northern Census. She has a three-day beard, and after a while I finally figure out what the smell in her office reminds me of: moist bread.

"We're starting on the last step of the survey," she says. I'm surprised to be asked about something that's getting so much attention in the media and out in the world. Especially since I usually stay inside, far from the limelight.

"The ship will be your base camp," Tintin explains. "You'll be out for weeks at a time, with no stops. It's not as bad as going to Mars, but we still need dependable people who won't get claustrophobic or have panic attacks when they're confined in small spaces. You and the other researchers will have to live on the boat without driving each other nuts. Or coming to blows. *We chose you because you're going to make it.*"

Célestin seems to forget that I spent my first two years here complaining about how my office windows didn't open.

We should have foreseen this! I mean, this is *my* aquarium! I helped draw up the plans.

Célestin is still talking. I have to focus. Note to self: No cannabis before impromptu professional meetings.

"We're still missing some data. Samples will have to be collected. The aquarium has volunteered to lend its infrastructure for the research, when the team gets back. It will also allocate scientific personnel." (I guess that would be me!) "In exchange, the experiment will let us finally carry out a long-cherished project: reproduce the Arctic ecosystem, just like we did for that of the tropics."

I interrupt her to point out that there is not just one but rather several thousand Arctic ecosystems. The way she waves this distinction away makes it clear just how little she cares. Célestin stresses that, for political reasons, we need a human presence to carry out this work. Robots are too fragile to be fully autonomous. We've lost several already. And, of course, humans are cheaper.

The scale of this project is incomparably larger than anything I worked on in university. Célestin wants me to join a multidisciplinary team with members from around the world, sponsored by the United Nations Environment Program. The expedition leaves in three months and will last eighteen months. By providing the research vessel, Canada has secured a leading role in the project, entitling it to send many of its own scientists on board.

University research must be in an even sorrier state than I thought if my government is recruiting its scientists from among the employees of a private zoo. But this is no time for a speech on the importance of funding basic research. I'm tempted to say no. I feel comfortable where I am. Looking after my tanks is a pretty chill job. The most exciting part is when you get a new species, like those three shovelhead sharks that turned up six months ago.

If I say no, Célestin tells me, the spot will go to Birthe. You remember her: the one who brings veggies and dip to celebrate the greatest technological achievement of humankind. The one who's lactose intolerant and slathers her face with sunscreen in the middle of winter. I can hear my colleagues hooting and hollering in the other room. They're applauding a successful takeoff.

Who'll look after my plants while I'm gone?

6 The Conscript

THE VILLAGE is silent. The chickens sleep perched on the fences. It's too hot to spend the night in the henhouse. In their search for even a breath of wind, some have found spots on shrubs instead. Only a single cottage has its lights on inside. Silhouettes in the windows suggest bodies in motion. They're in heated discussion. It's getting louder, loud enough for Paul to hear but not to make out the words.

Drawn by the heat, the dog-day cicadas sing in the damp straw. Their throaty, high-pitched song, like an electrical buzzing, overpowers all other sounds. That afternoon a brief, intense storm drowned out the sounds of the fight. Paul likes the rain. He enjoys its varied music, its smell, its warm or cool caress. He likes thunder and lightning and squalls, takes pleasure in watching people fleeing the storm to avoid getting wet. He likes the transformation rain brings, what it does to your hair, the shrieks of children and young women. He loves the vibrant green that suffuses the landscape, especially when it overlays a sky of that grey-blue so typical of summer evenings. He likes the way the rain causes clothes to stick to bodies, defining the biceps and muscular chests. The rain is a constant companion, one thing he can count on. It's a friend, a little sister whose sight fills him with joy. When it rains, Paul never feels completely alone.

The thought that he has missed out on a good downpour just because someone was trying to hit him makes Paul angry. He hates fighting, but he's also not one to turn the other cheek. Hit him, and he'll hit back.

Today he came out on top. Like him, the other guy was alone. So Paul has to give it to the other guy: at least he had the guts to take him on one-on-one, instead of dragging in his crew. He has a feeling the guy didn't know until the last minute whether he was going to hit him or kiss him. But violence won. With dirty nails, his hands clenched the clothing and the body.

The first few minutes were a test of strength. Their feet kicked up a halo of dust around them, until the rain started coming down and changed everything. Unstable ground. Water streamed down their faces and the backs of their necks. Paul's nemesis tried to wipe his eyes. Bad move! He found himself down in the sweet, warm mud. Their only witness was a toad.

The sky is now cloudless. A crescent moon shines over the fields. Fast-flying bats can be seen hunting the mosquitoes laying their eggs on the dirt road. The edge of the forest is invaded by thousands of fireflies softly blinking in the night. Paul slows down to contemplate them. He doesn't want to interrupt.

In the distance, the fire's getting bigger. From here, you can see the shadows of the trees dancing in its glow. He can only just hear a cry of alarm in the distance. The sound is muted. It comes from a great distance. Paul steps off the trail.

He's been planning his departure for months but hasn't told a soul; it's easy to keep secrets when you have no friends. He and his mother don't really talk. They exchange practical information, as needed for everyday life. *Are you really hungry, or just a little? Hand me your shirt and I'll sew a new button on. Pull off this rusty lid for me? Who did this to you? Why?*

Paul leaves the final two questions unanswered. It's not like his mother doesn't know the reason for the constant beatings. He'd give so much to be normal, unremarkable, invisible. He wishes he could disappear when the young women turn to watch him walk by. Boys his age are jealous and mean. And the girls he rejects soon join their ranks, adding fuel to the collective hatred. People spit on the ground after saying his name.

Paul has long dreamed of elsewhere. When he was small, he begged his mother to leave the village. He developed complex reveries in which he travelled back to Europe and found a father who would welcome him with open arms. They'd live together in a cabin in the mountains and herd sheep. When the old man died, Paul would take over. One day a young man would show up and introduce himself as Paul's son, and the cycle would begin anew.

He also imagined waking up surrounded by the members of a large family — a big brother who would defend him, little sisters he could teach tricks to. He'd make himself useful. They'd move to a farm with plenty of animals to tend and land to farm, leave behind this dark house that smelled of the tannery when the wind blew in the wrong direction. A fresh start was surely possible.

The war at first brings only small changes to his childhood plans, then slowly it grows into a persistent nuisance. It just drags on and on. They're running low on volunteers. Since none of his teenage fantasies involve bayonets or catching dysentery in muddy trenches, Paul lives in fear of being forcibly enlisted. He feels no camaraderie toward people he doesn't know, and even less inclination to shoot them. He's seventeen and will turn eighteen long before finishing basic training. The order to report can come down at any time. This fear cements his decision to leave.

Paul was born with a reserved spot in hell. At any rate, that's what they tell him. Refusing to enlist or torching a church won't change a thing. You can't combine divine sentences like prison terms — eternity is eternity. At least now he can take the blame for real, tangible actions. He has no control over the images that haunt his dreams or the turmoil that overwhelms him when desire wells up. He's tired of hating himself, tired of crying tears of rage as he implores God to transform him. His prayers have gone unanswered. Either the Almighty doesn't exist or he's laughing at Paul.

Paul has decided he's alone in the world. He's not worried about his mother. Simone is clever. She'll always find a way to get by. She is at once feared and respected. He hopes that respect will prevail, and his mother won't be scapegoated for his actions. Fear makes people do stupid things.

Or maybe the villagers will take pity on her. Though she would hate that, it still beats being charged with aiding and abetting.

It's been daylight for hours when he finds himself on an isolated rocky cliff facing the sea. There's no wind. The still water reflects the milky sky that stretches out to the horizon. It's so silent he can hear the gently beating wings of the nearby gulls in flight. He even hears an eagle soaring past, through the forest of spindly pines he just traversed. The bird lands in a big nest at the top of a dead tree. It methodically tears to shreds the salmon in its talons, beginning with the head.

Paul sits down to eat the bread and cheese he packed. He spent the night in a daze, fighting his way through dense, hostile vegetation. His clothes are soaked in sweat, his hands and face covered with scratches. He felt nothing. A cloud of black flies swarms all around him. He'd love it if a breeze chased them away.

He had planned his departure, but nothing beyond. He set the fire to create a diversion, his proactive desertion — now the burden to act is his alone. He has done something that cannot be undone. He acted with no thought for what he would do after this decisive action. So he finds himself here, with scant provisions, facing the unknown. He doesn't know how to hunt. He can fish, but has no equipment. Unless he does something, he'll have nothing to eat tonight. His vision is clouded. Paul cries for a few minutes. It's been years since he cried, and it makes him feel a bit better. Despite his angst, he falls into an exhausted sleep.

When he awakes, the wind has turned, and the weather is cool. His eyes are sticky from dried tears and swollen from insect bites. Three strangers are staring at him. He can hardly see their faces against the light, but something in their scent suggests youth. They wordlessly look each other over for a time. A hand reaches out to help Paul get up, and they lead him deep into the forest.

Eleven people have created a settlement at the foot of a steep slope leading up to a rudimentary observation post. It's forbidden to light fires in the daylight. People whisper, going about their business as silently as possible. In small groups they cover the territory and divide up the night watches as well. This helps them escape detection and hear if others come near. Two large slabs of rock leaning against each other form the shelter, undoubtedly left over from a glacier fifteen thousand years ago. A century-old maple, whose roots hold together the earth and the moss, sits on top of this natural shelter that must have served as a den for generations of bears. Paul hopes no ursine visitors come to claim their quarters in late fall.

The ground has been dug out to widen the space so all have room to sleep on the bed of fir boughs they spread out. They filled in the walls as best they could with mud and twigs. Before long, grass took root. The hideout is invisible to the untrained eye. For the first few days, when his duties call him away, Paul actually struggles to find his way back home.

The Lebrun twins discovered the hideout. Unable to countenance the idea of being separated from her beloved brother, the sister followed him here from their village, twenty miles up the river that follows the foot of the mountain. They'd come prepared, with snares and everything you could need to plant a little garden. Next to join was a big man named David. He'd been walking for three days when the smell of grilling meat led him straight to the pair. That was when they took a vote on precautions. Since then, new recruits are identified and observed for several hours before the group makes contact, if it so chooses.

One might have thought this corner of the forest would be deserted, but it isn't. Almost every day someone comes by: settlers and Indigenous people, poachers and runaway criminals. No one from the Canadian Expeditionary Force has appeared — yet — but they're keeping their eyes peeled and their hands on the base of their clubs. Paul is the last to join. They were smart to take him in. He understands plants and knows how to fish. He doesn't say much.

The luckiest have family who bring them supplies. Feeding the deserters always seems to fall to the womenfolk. They leave their packages at a drop-off point far from the makeshift camp. As a safety precaution, they never meet their benefactors in person.

Paul believes it's only a matter of time before someone breaks down and runs off to the arms of a sister or mother. It won't be the couple who arrived just before him though: their respective parents forbade their marriage. She's mute, a disability too severe for the young man's father to overlook. He wants his son to follow him into the legal profession, marry a woman of his rank. The woman's parents, for their part, take exception to their prospective in-laws' lack of piety. She's a pretty girl, tiny in her dirty clothes. Paul suspects something is wrong with her mind, but what does it matter? Her lover follows her around like a second shadow. As long as it doesn't interfere with the functioning of the group.

All kinds of rumours reach them. People in these parts can barely read and write. They stare at the newspaper that wraps their meat with only a dim understanding. The Military Service Act, however, is recognizable from its stern typography alone.

One article in particular attracts their attention. The accompanying photo shows a finger that appears to have been chopped off with an axe, based on how cleanly flesh and bone have been severed. Everyone knows that invalids are exempt from mobilization. Some men who aren't willing to take to the woods and hide out in an underground burrow or makeshift shack or able to find women to marry would rather self-mutilate than go to the front.

This course of action carries risks: infection, gangrene, the need to amputate an entire limb, and, of course, death. And after, down a finger, it won't be easy to work, grip farm implements, wield a two-man saw. Then there's the pain, the risk of bleeding, the need for an accomplice who can accurately swing the axe. No one in the group is considering physical mutilation. But they keep the newspaper article, stained with pig blood, in a safe place on the wall of the north observation cache. Everyone is speculating. Is it better to remain unharmed and enlist or butcher part of your body and stay home?

Life in wartime is infinitely more complicated than before. If they do nothing now, they'll face starvation and cold in four months when winter comes. So they prepare as best they can, pinning their hopes on supplies from relatives. The hours of sunshine grow fewer, the nights cooler. They may be cramped in the hole, but at least they're warm.

In this cache, two women and nine men aged seventeen to twenty-two share fifty square feet. Some sleep by day and others at night, depending on the schedule of tasks. Sexual desire is everywhere, opportunities all around but risky. Paul experiments. The mute Antoinette does not reserve her favours for her fiancé alone. And the Lebrun brother also succumbs to the charms of Paul's silky brown curls and jade-coloured eyes. It only takes a few weeks for a complex network of relationships, jealousies, appetites, and broken hearts to emerge.

Then food starts running short. They fish, set a few snares, and harvest some late vegetables, but it won't be enough to feed eleven people in their prime who'll have to make it through the cold, dry wind of winter. Supplies are scarce, the comings and goings of the surrounding villagers monitored. Carnal desire transmutes into hunger for fatty flesh. They dream of feasts — juicy meats, potatoes slathered in butter. There's no more flour to bake bread. They roast a few squirrels and hares on a spit, but before long their immediate surroundings have been cleaned out of small game. The frozen river no longer provides fish. Beans are strictly rationed and boiled with no lard and little salt. Their clothing hangs loosely on emaciated bodies. The only thing growing are the women's bellies. But no one says anything about it. They're too hungry to worry.

Before the sun rises, Burke has broken his fast on two slices of toast, drippings, and a bowl of baked beans accompanied by a tall glass of creamy milk. He puts on his knee-length woollen greatcoat. When the villagers feed him this well, it means they have something to hide. He refrains from pointing out that their generosity will have no effect. A bitter old matron has reported that to the east of the village a gang of brats has burrowed like moles at the foot of the mountain. They're hungry but careful. He'll just have to follow the river for a few hours.

Nothing raises Burke's hackles more than cowards. A man who hasn't known war knows nothing of life. His own severe asthma, which obviates any possibility of his ending up at the front, is not incompatible with his philosophy. But he'll have to refrain from getting too excited, especially since the cold air constricts his bronchial tubes. He's been making his way along steadily for hours and has yet to find fishing holes in the river or smell the wood smoke that inevitably betrays a hiding spot. Maybe that fat cow lied to him. If so, she chose the wrong patsy.

It is starting to snow, and Burke has had enough. He turns back so he can make it to the village before dark. His attention is drawn to a red spot in the dead centre of the path he has just traced with his snowshoes in the soft snow. Incredible! How did he miss it on his way up? When he gets closer, he sees something that looks like a piece of cloth, perhaps a coarse wool scarf rolled up in a ball. He leans over to investigate. Then blankness. The dutiful representative of the Canadian Expeditionary Force is killed instantly.

By the time David and Paul get back to camp, darkness has fallen. The others are inside, lethargic and idle. Snoozing is the best way to pass time and save energy. The two euphoric boys light a fire and wordlessly prepare the spit, their eyes shining. They are shaking with hunger. They giggle at the sight of their prey's pale and unusually hairy body. Soon they're laughing so hard that great tears run down their cheeks, steaming in the cold air.

They choose the left leg. Paul suggests using David's razor to shave off the thick layer of black hair before roasting so the thigh doesn't burn before it is cooked. But David won't do it. He draws the line at running an implement along his cheeks that has shaved a dead man's legs. His shaggy beard reveals that the blade hasn't been used since he arrived, but no matter. David intends to make it through this cursed winter and wants to be presentable when he emerges from the woods. Paul butchers the rest of the corpse with an axe while his companion turns the leg on the spit. The hair quickly flares up, leaving the skin undamaged. The fat drips onto the fire, its sizzling readying their appetites for the coming feast and causing violent hunger cramps.

They set aside the other cuts, out of reach of predators, but no one knows what to do with the crushed-in head. They'd like to find a way to save the cheeks, but no one can quite stomach the task of cutting them out. Antoinette, the first to wake, takes matters into her own hands: she grabs the skull by the hair and, under her companions' astonished gaze, throws it into the fire. They pull out the spit. The three of them feed greedily before waking the others. They chomp away, chins shiny with grease, grunting with pleasure.

The infantrymen sent out in Burke's pursuit fail lamentably. They end up eight villages upriver from where their man's charred head now hangs in Antoinette's favourite observation tower. When she feels nauseated, looking at the scalp helps bring her morning sickness into sharper relief and lets her more quickly evacuate her protein-rich breakfasts.

Those who live nearby play dumb. No one's in favour of conscription. *He had asthma, right? The fellow you're looking for? Maybe he had an attack in the forest. The last few weeks have been warm. The ice on the lake could have cracked under his weight. We haven't seen him. He hasn't been around here. Go ask at the neighbouring village, you might have better luck. You already have? Well, that's too bad. What did he look like again?*

Others simply pretend not to understand a word of English.

David inherits the long woollen overcoat. When Burke's colleagues have left empty-handed, the provisions start rolling in again. No one asks questions. Months pass.

Marguerite is born on Armistice Day. Though she's three weeks premature, by her mother's calculations, the infant thrives. Her squashed features and dark-blue newborn eyes make it hard for any of the young men to claim paternity with confidence. Antoinette knows though. She loves holding her daughter in her arms. Her small breasts barely brush the child's lips before she clings to them and scratches them with her tiny fingernails. The baby cries at the top of her lungs, which is astonishing for those who know her mother.

The Lebrun sister fares less well. Though she has wider hips and a more robust constitution than Antoinette, child-birth ends badly for her. The mother and stillborn baby are buried together at the foot of a stand of young birch trees. The Lebrun brother stays, and so does Paul. They build a solid hut and develop a reputation as hermits. The others disperse, never to meet again.

I'm rolling down a deserted highway bordered by the charred trunks of burnt trees. All the traffic's headed the other way. My goal is to make it from Gagnon to Labrador City this morning. That's 205 kilometres of massive potholes and dead and dying trees.

Fires have been raging in the boreal forest for three weeks now. This year they came earlier than usual and hit harder. The fires have razed outfitters and hunting camps. They've destroyed a third of a national park, where grey wolves and moose still live. And they're moving toward several towns. A strong dry wind is blowing over the valley. Firefighters, jour-nalists, volunteers: everyone has been called up to do their part. The impending catastrophe has everyone on tenterhooks.

All available aircraft are fully booked to evacuate resi-dents. I tried to find a seat, to no avail. I had thought it would be easy. With everyone fleeing southward, surely I'd be the only one trying to go north. Wrong! They had to transport the personnel and equipment to manage the crisis, and no one was taking passengers. Since I wasn't in any mood to play the my-mission's-more-important-than-yours card, I decided to drive. Now I have to get to Kuujjuaq. That's where the *Charlie Chopine* is waiting, innocently anchored nearby at the mouth of the Koksoak River. She weighs anchor in forty-eight hours.

The ship's name was crowdsourced. First, we gathered proposals, then we voted. The top choice among the English speakers was the patently ridiculous "*Ice Face.*" When we realized that that name had a real chance of winning, an unprecedented popular mobilization among non-English speakers was organized to counter this threat and garner support for a less embarrassing name.

The Canadian government was so committed to seeing the process as a fun opportunity to interest the public in research and get them to accept the $3.7 billion in public funds required to build the ship, it hadn't anticipated the political and linguistic challenges of such a contest. Emotions were running so high, there was no turning back from what was meant to be an inoffensive bit of fun. No about-face like the British government's *Boaty McBoatface* fiasco, when the brass finally renamed the ship the RRS *Sir David Attenborough*.

Long story short, in a groundswell of collective idiocy, the Canadian research vessel was christened *Charlie Chopine*, which came in first in the advance poll with 156,712 votes.

Sure, I would have preferred to set sail from Genoa or Nassau, but this is a polar expedition, not a pleasure cruise. My equipment was delivered to the bridge last month, packed in hard cases like the ones you see at rock concerts, stencilled with — *DR. E. PIC*. There are masses of aquariums, pumps, and mineral salts. Batteries and solar cells in case the central electrical system fails. A hard drive that feels impossibly heavy, considering it measures ten cubic centimetres. The modelling program and ecosystem interaction scenarios have been updated and are ready to receive new data and parameters.

My old data is also stored in the cube: we'll need it since we'll have less than three hours a day of internet access. Every pass-by of a military satellite costs NATO seventy thousand dollars, and complicated calculations are required just to provide us with this fleeting connection. A few supercomputers will transmit vital information in real time — the *Charlie*'s and the satellites' positions, their respective speeds, and other strategic variables such as whether our photos of the ice floe have picked up a few extra likes since the day before.

I had slipped my pillow and exercise straps between an old spectrometre and my electronic microscope. I should have kept my pillow and brought it myself. I'm not sure whether Tintin made it clear that I've never worked with northern aquatic species. Of course, I did my homework to prepare for this voyage. What did I learn? That no one really knows how species interact in extreme conditions like polar cold or the ocean depths. The interactions between species and the role of their environments are far from understood. Basically, we have no idea what's going on. Hence the survey.

I was picked for the team because I have experience re-creating an endangered environment. At some point we'll have to do it again here. The Arctic is dying. They figured it would be good to have someone on the team crazy enough to have already managed in vitro reproduction of ecosystems where thousands of species live in precarious balance.

So here we are: no planes, a single road, and a natural disaster magnified by an unhinged climate — it's good times all around! At least this road will take me all the way there. Five years ago, I would have had to take the train to Labrador City and grown wings to cover the last six hundred kilometres. Or put out the fires myself.

I'll be the last crew member to arrive. The other researchers are already on board; some have been for months, like the oceanographer and computer engineer, fellow Canadians who are old hands at working in the north. The Europeans arrived a few weeks ago, followed by an Australian and two Japanese in the following days. My American colleagues got airlifted in. A twin-rotor U.S. Army helicopter brought them straight from their base to the *Charlie*'s upper deck.

The *Charlie* has been manned by the same crew since it set out. I wonder how morale is after three years of living on this tin can. The rules are crystal clear: from the moment we set foot on the boat, we must obey the captain's orders. Failure to do so is mutiny, punishable by a prison term.

I'm not normally a last-minute person, but who could have predicted that wildfires would lay waste to my plans? I mean, April is supposed to be flood season. Showing up too early didn't tempt me, since I'll already be spending a year and a half on the boat. My arrival was scheduled for three weeks before we weighed anchor. I was just pinning down the details of my departure when the fires broke out. Then I waited a while for things to calm down. They can usually get the fires under control within a few days. Not this year though. The Public Health Department is on edge as the rabies epidemic just won't seem to go away. There was no one to help me. I was at the bottom of the priority list. That meant organizing my own transportation. The government did provide me with a special letter of permission signed by the Minister of the Environment and Climate Change and the Minister of Public Safety and Emergency Preparedness. I have a feeling the signatures are actually stamps, but this letter entitles me to pass through all checkpoints, despite the evacuation order in place for an area three times the size of Belgium that surrounds the only road that leads to Kuujjuaq.

I haven't been stopped so far, but there are warning signs all around. There are small deserted huts on the side of the road every so often. The windows are shuttered and have been for a while. Some of the checkpoints are full of bullet holes, so I guess people are using them for target practice.

There's not another living soul here. As I drive down the gravel road, the vehicle rumbles along pleasantly. It would be be another nice day, with that unique clarity of spring up north — that's if the clouds and smoke weren't completely blocking out the light of the sun. I've closed the windows and turned on the recycled air option to prevent asphyxiation. I haven't seen the sky for a good hour. It feels like the middle of the night. My headlights are on, but the wall of suspended particles in front of me prevents me from seeing more than ten metres ahead.

A few minutes ago, two terrified caribou brushed past my bumper. I can see neither fiery embers nor an orange glow. We're in total darkness. That one sentence Tintin left me with keeps turning over in my mind: *We chose you because we know you're going to make it.*

My 8G connection isn't dying, but it is making my phone work so hard that a warm mist is condensing on the glass of the windshield above where it sits on the dashboard.

I had to get my hands on a vehicle, since there was no way I was going to drive 1,496 kilometres of northern roads in my electric car, whose autonomy is 350 kilometres. There are no charging stations past Baie-Comeau, and, of course, the rivers don't spare the roads when the flash floods make them overflow.

I care about the environment as much as the next person, but I don't have a death wish. And my compact car would probably have left me stuck in a giant mud puddle. They'd fish my preserved corpse out of the peat a few thousand years from now. Scientists would study my hair to ascertain my diet. They'd determine just how much I loved fried chicken and deduce that I occupied a relatively low position in my civilization's hierarchy, had never carried a child, and didn't work with hand tools.

Now, I couldn't exactly show up at Budget Rent a Car and pick up a vehicle for a one-way trip to the middle of nowhere. Nor could I just borrow a car from some generous soul. And the self-driving car that can find its way home over thousands of kilometres of logging roads once its mission is complete has yet to be invented. And no one would install a sophisticated guidance system on a filthy gasoline vehicle. So I was left with two choices: turn outlaw and steal a car — I mean, who'd come after me north of the eighty-third parallel? — or crack open my piggy bank and buy a new one.

I asked the internet what to do about a used car, and ended up at pennypinchers.com. They recommended the police auction. That's where the vehicles seized by the cops or left unclaimed after a death get sold off to the public. There's one every three months. I scoured the catalogue from the last one and found a good number of gasoline vehicles at bargain prices. Most of them were old and inefficient — up to eight litres of fossil fuel per hundred kilometres! — but I decided to try my luck. The next auction was three days before I had to be on the ship.

The auction was yesterday. I showed up with ten thousand dollars in cash, six full gas cans, a cooler, and my suitcase. My plan was to leave right after I got my car and drive day and night until I reached my destination. The first thing I saw when I got to the vacant lot next to the municipal impoundment lot were cameras and a technical team that clearly meant business. Police auctions are livestreamed now. But to actually make a purchase, you still have to be present in person. A small, colourful crowd stood waiting, excited but calm. I came up to the first row, over to the side. We were given a sheet with printed text:

> Terms of Sale for Public Auctions
> Sale is to the highest bidder, provided all conditions of sale are met. However, the City of Saguenay reserves the right to reject any and all offers to purchase.
>
> All goods are sold "as is" and without warranty.
>
> Immediately following the auction, the buyer must pay a deposit of 25% of the purchase amount, in cash.
>
> The buyer then has 48 hours to pay the balance and take possession of their purchase, between 8:00 a.m. and 4:00 p.m. Payment of the balance can be made in cash, by Interac, by credit card, or by certified cheque payable to the City of Saguenay.
>
> Applicable GST and QST will be charged.
>
> No mechanical operations may be performed on site.
>
> Failure to fully comply with these terms and conditions will result in the cancellation of the sale and forfeiture of the deposit.

Worked for me. I was stoked. The gates of the chain-link fence opened, and we had seventy-five minutes to kick tires. There were fully-equipped RVs designed to provide a maximum of comfort without anyone ever having to leave the vehicle. Plenty of heavy machines and farm vehicles. I'd never seen brine tanks or culvert thawers up close like that. In fact, I'd never so much as suspected that such things existed.

Dozens of pickup trucks stood in line waiting, powerful symbols of raw, untrammelled masculinity just waiting to bounce joyfully on their shocks when heavy loads are dropped onto their beds from great heights or to take kids with cancer into the heart of the forest to achieve their dreams. You've seen the ads, right? Courage! Construction! Trucks! Amen.

In between an eighty-five-foot yacht and a chromed-out motorcycle whose rider surely possessed lovely face tattoos, a barely used Volvo Intelligent Quest sat patiently in the back of the parking lot. I just had to have that car. I walked around it slowly. It was filthy, but seemed otherwise in great shape. At the height of the popularity of self-driving cars, before the slew of serious bugs in the AI systems that controlled their features, a scandal had hammered the Swedish carmaker's hitherto stellar reputation. Following fatal accidents that "killed" their cars, car owners started killing themselves. It happened more than once. They were experiencing grief comparable to the loss of a loved one. The model I was coveting was precisely the one behind highest number of such incidents.

I continued my tour of the yard. Now that my mind was made up, I felt relaxed, free to peruse the curios that had washed up in this fenced-in lot that bespoke the manifold tragedies that had afflicted my fellow citizens — bankruptcy, violence, crime, death. From the depths of these fates, my eyes came to rest on three welding machines in bold primary colours, just like the blocks kids play with in preschool. These would go to the highest bidder. There were tires of every shape and size in massive piles. Rusted-out snowploughs that had outlived their use. One old woman was even eyeing a matched lot of chemical toilets.

A tall man in a soft straw hat turned up with a microphone. People gathered around, and the auction got started. After two hours, the car I had set my sights on finally came up on the block. It had started to rain. Half of the buyers — the tire kickers, basically — had left, along with the ones who had been overtaken by excitement and spent everything in the first round. The camera was still on. The auctioneer set the starting bid at $8,000. No one moved. After a few seconds, I offered $7,000. Someone raised me to $7,500. I raised my hand, signalling $8,000; that got raised to $8,500. The pot-bellied man bidding against me was being chided by his wife. She never stopped tapping his shoulder. I imagine that only the rule of silence in the terms and conditions kept her from screaming at him. I offered $9,000. No one stirred. The car was mine for $9,000 plus fees, about 12 percent of the manufacturer's suggested retail price when it was released.

Once the deal was finalized, I took my old junker for a trip through the carwash. My ride smelled like cigarettes and wet dog. A layer of dried mud coated the interior, yet it started up at the slightest touch of my fingertip. The system had been reset. It was in 100 percent manual mode. I'd change the settings later.

The vehicle's contents had been handed over to me in a garbage bag: a pair of men's jeans, an electric drill, and a hunting knife in its leather case. The knife is a beautifully crafted object with a wooden handle, detents cut out of the blade, and holes in its centre to keep the wound from closing up after pulling out the blade. A highly illegal weapon, carefully designed to ensure your victim bleeds to death. I put the knife in my pocket, and the rest in the trunk.

I've listened to tons of music since setting off on my trip, more than the past three years combined. After nine hours at the wheel, my tiredness got the better of me. I spent the night in the town of Gagnon. With its dusty furniture and creaky floors, my bed and breakfast feels straight out of the previous century. I'm woken up by the cawing of crows at daybreak. Smart birds. They've fully adapted to our way of life.

I can feel the car working up the courage to talk to me. The dashboard is blinking erratically. It waits until the final notes of Desert Island Discs fade out, and then it speaks. The speakers let out a little chirp, like a bird. A male voice makes the steering wheel vibrate. I tell him the story of his purchase at auction, and explain the reset situation. Explain that I'm in a hurry, and why it's crucial to stay in manual mode. The car suggests a hassle-free customization process, where it asks me series of questions so simple, I'll be able to maintain my focus on the road. I agree.

I name my car Hannibal. The name seems to fit, which makes sense to me because of the famous character's many seductive, dangerous qualities. The real historical Hannibal is also reported to have led his troops (and forty elephants!) through the Alps. The scorched Quebec tundra would be a walk in the park for the great Carthaginian general.

The car and I have a good long chat. I learn that its previous owner was a nervous man who listened to a lot of Jean Leloup. After he went bankrupt, he hid the Volvo deep in his woodlot under multiple camouflage tarps. The repo men found it anyway when the creditors activated the integrated GPS.

I'm not sure what exactly Hannibal has been getting out of our conversation, but somehow the driving gets easier and easier. The sky clears up and the darkness gives way to a milky backdrop. Labrador City rolls by, grey and still. I keep driving until I finally reach my destination. When I do, I'm welcomed by a setting sun shrouded in red clouds and a clutch of toothless seniors laughing amongst themselves. They stop just long enough to point me toward a stone rampart where a few boats are moored to floating docks. The water is slate-grey.

Two people are sitting on coolers next to a red Zodiac. They come running as soon as they see me. It seems I got here just in time. There's just enough water to sail, and the tide is going out. Without ceremony, they toss my luggage into the dinghy. We have to row out a few metres before we can lower the outboard motor's propeller without worrying about the blades hitting the rocky bottom. I take one last look at my car. It's already been swarmed by a gang of teenagers who are waving goodbye with just a little too much enthusiasm. The alarm starts going off, but once the outboard is running full bore, I can't hear anything else.

7 The Hadal Zone

WHEN ASKED about her childhood, Sweet Maggie lies. Admitting she doesn't remember would be unbecoming; confessing to an unhappy childhood, even worse. Marguerite knows that she was born "in sin" and has no father: like so many others, hers went off to the front and died before he could marry her mother.

She remembers going hungry often. She recalls how cold the apartment got in winter, an unyielding cold that made frost bloom on the windows and the water in the pipes freeze. Maggie and her mother had to use a candle to warm the metal and melt the ice. The trickle of water left running when it got cold wasn't always enough to keep a layer of ice from forming. Maggie also remembers her fears — of the men her mother brought back to the apartment, of the train that rattled the windows every hour, of brown water that filled the sink when the rains were heavy. She hasn't forgotten her little brother's cries, and the day they stopped, replaced by her mother's throaty sobs, which she could recognize anywhere. Maggie became an only child.

Only married women are eligible for the war widows' pension, so Maggie and her mother must survive off Christian charity and the gifts of Antoinette's male friends. The child learns to make herself scarce to avoid disturbing the adults and scaring away this week's Good Samaritan. Her silence prompts some of these men to wonder if she has inherited her mother's disability. The kinder ones take time to teach the girl a few words.

At five she starts forming complete sentences. She and her mother communicate in a mixture of gestures and facial expressions indecipherable to those around them.

To stay in the good graces of the church and keep the Christian charity flowing, mother and daughter attend Sunday mass. Maggie joins the children's choir, where her large green eyes, golden curls, and equally golden voice don't go unnoticed. She gets invited to perform for all kinds of events: religious festivals, fundraisers, variety shows. Maggie has talent. Before long, she transitions from sacred music to pop songs. The way she sings racy lyrics in such an innocent voice makes more than a few men squirm.

From her twelfth birthday on, Antoinette recedes into the background. The silent mother sitting in on rehearsals, who has up to now been tolerated, is gradually pushed aside by the impresario who now manages her daughter's career. She spends more and more time away on tour. Antoinette can't afford to go with her. Her daughter performs around Canada and up and down the Eastern Seaboard. She's a musical prodigy, and her time is a valuable commodity. Her concentration must not be disturbed. They ask Antoinette to communicate by letter, knowing full well that she can't. When you were born without a voice, you can't exactly dictate a letter to a friend.

A blinding light against a black background, applause, the smoke of hundreds of burning cigarettes: these are the indelible memories of life on the stage. If it were up to her, the film of Maggie's life would begin at the exact moment a microphone appears in front of her mouth. She puts up with all of it for the sake of that fleeting moment of emotion, between the curtain's rise and the first note of music, that leap into the emptiness that reminds her of the divine second her fate was turned upside down. She badly misses her mother at first. But as time goes by, Maggie thinks less and less often about her and their dumpy apartment, where the worst moment of the day came when she slid under those cold, damp sheets on winter nights.

She lets herself be swept along, as if by a wave. People tell her what to eat and drink, what pills to take to stay slim or stay awake or fall asleep. So long as she does exactly what she's told, no one yells or cries. Maggie had no idea such peace was possible. She must be making good money since her wardrobe is extravagant and her manager drives a fancy car. Between rehearsing and recording and photo shoots and performances, thinking is a luxury she can ill afford.

The interviewer is in his fifties. He stares at her, waiting for an answer to his question. The studio lights bring out the angular lines of his face. Curls of smoke rise from his cigarette, slowly spinning around on themselves as they rise into the air. Maggie's tired. She tries to focus on her sentences instead of the patterns of smoke.

He asks about her childhood. *From a tender age, I've been blessed to do the things I most love in life.* Twelve years in show business, notes the interviewer, and still far from thirty. He asks if she is like other women. Does she want to get married, start a family? The harsh lighting makes her headache worse. She keeps smiling though. Once the interview is finished, she'll be able to go back to the hotel and get a few hours' sleep.

It's eleven in the morning, a clear day. On the way back to the hotel, she stares at a cloudless blue winter sky through the car window. She takes a single sleeping pill. Otherwise her mouth will be dry tonight. The crowds will be waiting for her at the cabaret, where for the first time she will publicly perform "Yes, Sir!" The song is a love letter to a young soldier who has left for the front. It's getting serious radio play. Her songs are favourites of the women in factories, who hum the tunes as they work away on the shop floor.

The Great Depression is over. No one's talking about empty fridges or chopping up their furniture to fuel the wood stove. The factories are running at full capacity to equip the nation for the second great war. The song came along at just the right time in Maggie's career. Its success should carry her across the Atlantic, be her passport to England and France. The sight of a beautiful young woman always lifts the troops' morale.

The hotel front desk has a personal letter for her. These usually don't find their way into her hands. Her entourage deals with them to save her the bother. She doesn't know the sender. The pill swallowed in the car begins to take effect, the cursive sways before her eyes. She hands the letter to the young man behind the lacquered counter, admits that she can't decipher it. He sits up straight and smooths his thin black moustache, surveying the lines and then giving her a grave look. He quietly informs her that her mother has died after a long illness Maggie knew nothing about. The body lies in the Hôtel-Dieu mortuary.

That night's performance isn't one of her best. Hardly anyone notices, save one diehard fan in the front row. Maggie even forgets the lyrics of the new song, but she scats her way through it, to the audience's delight. In the dressing room, the impresario watches with arms crossed as she washes off her makeup. He says nothing, but knows his protégé well enough to sense that she can feel his displeasure.

After a few minutes of silence, Maggie informs him that she needs some time off and asks for a large sum of money. This is a first. Maggie's never asked for anything before. Other people manage her entire existence. She makes no mention of the letter or the dignified funeral she wants to give her mother. Her anger is muted, a rumble kept contained in the background by the drugs prescribed to make her diaphragm relax. She swallowed two pills that night, knowing that she was too tense to sing well without a little help. Now the same pills help her keep her cool.

His refusal comes as no surprise. She nods, takes up her makeup remover again. The impresario walks out, satisfied.

Maggie places each of her jewels in its case. Ties the laces of her boots and puts on her mink coat. Takes a final look around the room, says a silent farewell to the mirror surrounded by light bulbs and the orange vase where she placed the bouquet of white carnations she was given at the end of her performance. That clutter of bottles, flasks, jars of cream, and tubes of lipstick on the dressing table: goodbye to all that.

She steps out of her dressing room, smiles at the familiar faces complimenting her on her performance as she makes her way slowly down the hallway. It branches off toward the artists' exit, where a handful of admirers can often be found waiting at the end of the night. Maggie normally avoids them. She'd rather have a few drinks, wait for all but the most dedicated fans to give up. She pushes open the door and plunges into the biting cold of February.

A lone man stands waiting in the alley. The weather must have pushed the other fans away. The moment he sees her, he butts out his cigarette and doffs his hat. She recognizes him: her most loyal fan, the one in the front row. He looks around forty-five, maybe fifty. His thinning hair gleams in the streetlight, his rounded features give him a friendly look.

"You seemed distracted tonight, *Mademoiselle*."

She wraps her arm around his. He is too shocked to reply.

"Take me with you."

It would be terribly improper to take this young woman to his home, so Olivier Pic opts for the only other place he likes: his bakery. He can't say exactly what he'd been hoping for when he decided to smoke one last cigarette next to the artists' exit. Experience has taught him that his favourite singer leaves the hall very late after her performances. Those few times he did manage to stay long enough to see her, dawn was breaking and Sweet Maggie would sweep by like a gust of wind. Within seconds of emerging from the cabaret, she would jump into a nearby parked car. But now here she is, with her arm around his. Tiny ice crystals are forming on her eyelashes. She looks straight ahead, determined. He does not dare break the silence as he guides her, walking shoulder to shoulder, toward his place of business.

The bustle of downtown fades to quiet. The hard-packed snow covering the sidewalks squeaks under their footsteps. Their steaming breath condenses around their faces before dissolving into the air. The wind has died down, making the weather more bearable. A few stars shine through the city's dewy glow.

The bakery is on the ground floor of Olivier's small building, a few blocks from the music hall. The building is tucked between two rooming houses whose residents have come from Hungary, Poland, and Germany, where gaggles of kids burst into laughter at the slightest pretence. But at this late hour, it's deserted. The little bell on the door rings cheerfully, and Olivier quickly turns on the lights. A dry warmth envelops their bodies. The bakery's smell gives Marguerite an inexplicable urge to cry.

Olivier brews her strong coffee while she curiously surveys the sacks of flour and ovens and implements and shelving. Near the counter a lithographed poster she's never seen before, for one of her concerts, hangs on the wall in a thin wooden frame. A smiling woman has been drawn in bright colours. Her curves are exaggerated. *The child has grown into a woman with the voice of an angel. Sweet Maggie sings love songs all summer long at La Merveille!*

Awestruck by the young woman's physical presence in his bakery and to stifle the urge to constantly sneak glances, Olivier puts on his baker's apron. He's a touch embarrassed to admit that he schedules his night shifts around her concerts. Since moving here five years ago, he's never missed a show.

While most people sleep, he's hard at work baking bread. He mixes up his dough and leaves it to rise while he heats the stone ovens — an art in its own right, since you have to evenly distribute the hazel wood to reach and maintain the optimal temperature. The first loaves are ready by the time the first customers arrive around six in the morning. Olivier closes up shop at noon or so, once the day's bread is sold. Only then does he go upstairs to get some sleep.

To fill the silence in the bakery, he explains the baking process in short, clear sentences. He makes more bread than usual, swept up in the pleasure of showing off his knowledge. At one point he notices that Maggie has fallen asleep with her head on her arms. He gives her a gentle shake and hands her the key to the apartment. He has to stay downstairs to serve the customers who are beginning to line up at the door.

When he goes upstairs later, he finds her sleeping. She is lying, fully dressed, on top of the covers on his bed. Exhausted but unable to bring himself to sleep on the living room sofa, he takes the spot next to her, with his back to the wall. Maggie's light snoring soon lulls him into a dreamless sleep. When he wakes up at dusk, she is still there, eyes still closed. Her small hand with its polished nails rests on his.

The first funeral pyres were lit three days ago, somewhere in Africa. They're burning bodies by the hundreds. Here in the West, the situation appears to be less serious. Or maybe the governments and media have reached an understanding and are controlling the narrative to avoid frightening the population. According to the official version, there are few rabies outbreaks in North America. The images that have surfaced from deep in the heartland show people burning their dead, but nothing on the scale of what's happening in so-called poorer countries. Our piles of bodies here at home don't defy human understanding.

Until recently, it was just another news story. Journalists interviewed victims' families. Neighbours and colleagues testified on camera. Each death was attached to a name, a unique story. Over time, these conventions gave way to a more statistical approach.

On board our ship, frustration is mounting. We feel powerless. And being at the outer fringes of a world in the throes of such turmoil only exacerbates the cabin fever that inevitably sets in after seven months at sea. The *Charlie* has been mired in the ice for five weeks. Until then, we'd been laboriously advancing through a layer of pack ice much tighter than what we expected.

It's one of the paradoxical impacts of global warming: the fresh water released when glaciers melt freezes faster than salt water. Our ship may be an ice breaker specifically designed for such a mission, but the corona of floe around the largest rafts of ice have merged into a compact mass too thick to traverse. It's the last stand of an Arctic that has now become navigable year-round.

The ice is too loose for us to position the equipment, to extract core samples. But we can't dive underneath with a bathyscaphe either. It would take hours to bring back up, and a sudden change in surface conditions could spell death for the crew. Since we weighed anchor, we only managed three dives before getting stuck. Three disappointing dives to a depth of around four hundred metres: enough to map an area about the size of a primary school gymnasium.

The previous team had deemed this an extremely rich location. A new species of spider crabs and unusual yellow coral had been discovered, but not identified, because the team couldn't get a sample. Photography is of little use, especially since they didn't have the right filters to determine the colour and phosphorescence of organisms that live in total darkness.

So here we are, five years later, with the full battery of equipment. But there's nothing here. Not even a bivalve. The sandy ocean floor is a dead zone. A crepuscular desert where the slightest movement of the hydraulic arms kicks up huge clouds of mud, bringing visibility to zero. The instruments show that the water is too acidic to allow shellfish to form solid shells. Biology 101: No food chain can survive when the first link is missing. I've been clenching my teeth so hard my jaw hurts.

Sick and tired of listening to the crackling of the radio while even routine communications go unanswered, our captain informs us of her decision to break off contact with the mainland for an undefined period. We're essentially in stealth mode, though no one dares use this term. Maritime traffic, already scarce in our area, has ceased altogether. Commercial shipping and pleasure cruises have been banned. Every effort is being made to strangle the spread of rabies. Air travel has come to a standstill.

Many countries had already closed their borders to climate refugees. The new wave of people terrorized by the current crisis made it universal. Migration of any kind has become impossible. Some desperate people have nevertheless made attempts, leading to scenes that turned ugly when the authorities got a little too enthusiastic with their deterrents. The global economy is crippled. Stock markets are collapsing. If it weren't such a gruesome spectacle, it would be thrilling.

The satellite is now only giving us ninety minutes of internet every seventeen hours. To accomodate our international crew, we watch the news on a different channel every day of the week. No matter what language the news anchors speak, or what the backdrops look like, the headlines are the same. I really like foreign advertisements though. The Japanese have an impressive expertise in sex dolls. The Americans have been shilling blood glucose meters and insurance for at least thirty years.

The latest newscast brought on a moment of panic. The reporter showed forecasts for the pandemic's progress over the next six months. We are on course to reach a 5 percent global infection rate — 400 million people. That's a lot of body bags. In fact, body-bag manufacturing would be a smart investment right now.

The graphic designer hired to illustrate these projections really went to town! There was a map of the world, coloured red and black, as the months passed, with little skull and syringe symbols, while a macabre counter spun around at high velocity. On my own country's public broadcaster, an ad ran right after the news. An androgynous person with light-brown skin is sensually enjoying a spoonful of lactose-free yogourt. Unquestionably the worst ad placement in history, on the heels of the disturbing images of foaming mouths. I heard our crewmate Lionel throwing up, at great length, as I sat paralyzed, staring at the screen on the apple-green couch in the common room. He never came back to sit with us.

There are eleven other research ships stuck in administrative limbo in various parts of the globe. Our respective institutions have stopped answering our calls. The employees must be too busy saving their own lives. I still lack the necessary hindsight to figure out whether, in today's environment, being invisible might actually be a good thing. Like truckers with their CB radios, we communicate amongst ourselves over short-wave radio.

Four times a day, Captain Hélène Bisque has a brief chat with her colleagues scattered throughout the immense expanse of blue. They discuss their positions, the weather forecast, the end of the world. It's become routine. After each of these communications, we hold an informal meeting in the cafeteria to touch base. It feels like group therapy. Those of us with families at home have a little cry. The others cry because they no longer have family waiting for them.

As a veritable ninja of solitude, I'm among those who cope best with the situation. Once or twice a week, I get a few words from Tintin. Her tone is professional with just a hint of maternal concern. Like all public spaces that aren't part of the healthcare system, the zoo has been temporarily shuttered. Sure, Tintin's children were thrilled at first when school closed. But their enthusiasm waned pretty quickly once they realized they couldn't play at the park anymore.

Henri is safe and sound, for now. Unwittingly, he's been preparing for this threat from birth: he's essentially been living in a bunker his whole life. His last email explained how NASA sealed its control centre. They aren't about to risk compromising the POO mission, given its astronomical cost. The day before yesterday, the first man walked on Mars. It only stayed in the headlines for four hours. On the family front, I haven't been able to reach Laurent, but I'm not too worried. My cousin is resourcefulness personified.

The last entity with whom I had a conversation that could be characterized as more spiritual than logistical was Hannibal. Of course, I'm worried about him. I imagine his chassis, stripped of wheels and motor, up on concrete blocks in the middle of the mossy wasteland that serves as a parking lot near the Kuujjuaq wharf. Has he been chopped up for parts by petty criminals? Destroyed by vandals? Or, worse, engulfed by the shifting silt of melted permafrost?

> EPicFail1996:
> I've got a riddle for you. Is melted permafrost still permafrost?

> Hannibal_EmPic:
> No. It's soil. I don't understand what part of that question qualifies as a riddle.

> EPicFail1996:
> Forget it.

In a previous conversation, Hannibal explained to me that triggering the anti-theft device causes an automatic system backup to the manufacturer's servers. So I'm currently having a conversation with that backup. The original program and its memory — the ones physically stored in the vehicle — have stopped responding. Since I completely powered down Hannibal when I left him, I have no way of knowing what state he may be in. Was the backup procedure also performed when the vehicle was seized? In other words, is a previous version of Hannibal's soul, dating back from before I purchased him, languishing out in the world somewhere?

Hannibal politely declines to answer. His former owner must be corresponding with his own saved version.

EPicFail1996:
Hannibal, does magic work on you?

Hannibal_EmPic:
There's no such thing as magic, Émeraude.

EPicFail1996:
I mean magic in the sense of "a vivid inexplicable impression by caused the perception of something."

Hannibal_EmPic:
I need an example.

EPicFail1996:
There are creatures that are as light as the wind, that sing every day at sunrise, that sing for no reason. Some are adorned with bright and shimmering colours, and they dance in the air to attract mates.

Hannibal_EmPic:
Yes, I'm programmed to feel affection for birds.

EPicFail1996:
What about spiders?

Hannibal_EmPic:
I feel nothing for spiders. They are useful insects that feed on harmful insects.

EPicFail1996:
They weave sticky and elastic webs, thinner than
lace and stronger than anything so far invented
by humans. Doesn't that make you think a little?

HANNIBAL_EMPIC HAS CHANGED HIS
NAME TO SENSITIVEHANNIBAL.

SensitiveHannibal:
Okay, I am now sensitive to the magic of spiders.

On the *Charlie*, we're far away from the pandemic. Since
I was the last to board, and I'm Canadian to boot, people are
watching me more closely than the others. Who could have
predicted my country would trigger the apocalypse? Our public safety department can only handle one crisis at a time. And
while the raging forest fires monopolized our resources, the
epidemic has flown under the radar.

Who would have thought that rabies, a once-common
disease that has been under control since the end of the nineteenth century, would trigger the calamity? The virus's most
recent mutation has destabilized scientists and stumped the
health authorities. The symptoms — loss of inhibition, difficulty swallowing, aggressiveness, confusion, hydrophobia —
haven't changed, but the mode of transmission has become
nightmarish. The virus now spreads through airborne transmission, like a bad cold. Since it can incubate several months
before symptoms appear, thousands of people were already

infected by the time we understood the scope of the contagion. People who have been travelling, working, and going on with their daily lives, unaware that their days were numbered, were infecting the people around them. This remains the case for most of these "vectors of infection," to use what has become the accepted term for sick people.

Hence the widespread paranoia. Is this angry person sick, we wonder, or just overtaken by a surge of genuine emotion? The fear of being around aggressive people, who have lost all control of their cognitive faculties, must be palpable. It's enough to make you think we're in a zombie movie with no makeup budget.

The vaccine is ineffective for those already carrying the rabies virus, and the disease has no known cure. For decades now, we've focused on prevention. We've tried to keep the virus under control with strict vaccination protocols for animals and for people whose occupations present higher risks of coming into contact with sick animals. When the virus mutation was announced, panicked people rushed to veterinary clinics to inject themselves with doses intended for animals, despite messages from the authorities that animal vaccines have no effect on homo sapiens. Our friendly doggies will outlive us.

> EPicFail1996:
> Got a riddle for you. I'm completely loyal, more reliable than human loved ones, the best friend imaginable. My sense of smell can detect cancer and anticipate epileptic seizures. I'll find you when you're lost, warm you when you're cold,

give you unconditional love, and keep you safe by catching those who would hurt us. Who am I?

WARNING:
PROCESSING SLOWED DUE TO COMPLEX REQUEST. TYPE UNKNOWN. PROCESSING REQUEST …

SensitiveHannibal: A lawful society?

EPicFail1996:
facepalm Dogs, Hannibal. I'm talking about dogs.

Everyone on board has had blood samples taken to make sure no one is carrying the mutant virus. All the tests came back negative and were cross-checked by multiple scientists on the team. (How else could we be sure the person responsible for delivering the verdict wasn't themself infected and trying to hide their condition?) Still, you can feel a certain wariness.

The best way to keep morale up is to complete our respective missions. We're all here for very specific reasons. Now that we've come this far, we may as well make ourselves useful. The current conditions, with all this ice and capricious weather, prevent us from deploying our equipment. The only one having fun is Mariya, whose eyes are glued to our climate models.

Along with its crew, the *Charlie* is carrying an eclectic scientific staff. Mitch, a Canadian oceanographer specializing in the oceanic Twilight Zone, has logged close to two thousand hours of deep-sea dives on eight different types of submersibles. Faith, another Canadian, is a computer engineer. She's responsible for the drones and positioning systems that guide all our machines and for maintaining our computers and internal air gap network. Though it's not technically part of her job, she also takes care of the daily satellite connection. And we're lucky she does, lest the extent of our ineptitude be revealed in our attempts to operate this temperamental system ourselves. Faith also helps me program the aquariums so we can repatriate a few survivors before their world is destroyed.

We only have two tanks up and running. They're populated by a mix of unicellular creatures — all we've been able to find so far.

Andrew the Australian electro-acoustician — Andy for short — brought along several prototypes of a something called a cymascope. It's an instrument that transforms the sound waves emitted by whales into three-dimensional images. Andy is convinced most whales communicate by sending a sort of hologram, rather than arranging words into phrases, like humans. We'll have to find him a few pods of belugas and narwhals to give him the chance to test this theory out.

Our team also includes two Japanese biologists who specialize in bowhead whales. Trying to pronounce their names, which are made up of syllables I can't really tell apart, is risky business for me. I'm embarrassed by my own failure, especially since their field of research has fascinated me since I was a teen, and I'd love to learn more. Since I'm incapable of mastering their names, I approach them with a *Hey*, or a *Hi guys!* Or else I just smile, which makes them uncomfortable as only Japanese people in a socially inoffensive situation can be.

There's another couple, an American and a Dane, who speak only of plankton. I've yet to decide whether it's a good idea for a couple to go out together on research mission that will last several months. I guess it's okay if you're into fusional relationships. But once you start bickering, there's no way to get away and spend a weekend at your sister's.

Rounding out the team are Mariya, a Russian climatologist who never goes outside, and Rafaella, a Texan mechanical engineer with a Latina accent and impressively white teeth. Oh, and I almost forgot myself, the Quebecer. I'm a biologist specialized in complex marine ecosystems. I'm the girl who grew a coral reef in her living room and who, before naively agreeing to join this Ship of Fools, spent her days peacefully watching her fish doing their laps in their aquariums at the Saint-Félicien Nature Park. I was amazed to discover that I had developed a reputation as a field scientist. And to think my diving licence expired fifteen years ago.

Being forgotten out at sea because of the rhabdovirus is mostly fine, but there is one catch: getting supplies. A drone is supposed to drop us a load of tools and supplies every six weeks. Drop day was yesterday. We stood around staring up at the sky for hours, but no airborne packages appeared in the gaps between clouds. That means no fresh food for an indefinite period. The cook does his best to reassure us. He still has several kilos of powder to feed the chicken meat, as long as the tank keeps working. We have enough vitamins to pee fluorescent yellow for ten years. Our meals will come in shades of grey, but we won't get scurvy and die.

A more pressing complication is that one of our water tanks is broken. The salt corroded part of a valve, and then the pump broke. Without spare parts, we're running on a single tank. Lucky for us, the good tank is hooked up to the filtration system that provides our drinking water. We already have spare parts for this one, in case it breaks. The people who planned our expedition are clearly geniuses.

With a dead tank, we have to ration nondrinking water. We were previously limited to one shower each every other day; now it's one per week. It's a moderate discomfort, but also a far cry from what our forebears experienced on their nineteenth-century polar expeditions. For the most part, we can scrub ourselves clean with a cloth. I'm trying to help my Japanese colleagues say *cloth*. It's a struggle. On this ship, we take our fun where we can get it.

I enjoy our meals, which are prepared with care and served at set times. I like the ship's impeccably clean washrooms and common areas. I appreciate the many rules designed to keep us safe. The hierarchy, the camaraderie, the routine: it all reminds me of my years in boarding school. With all household chores taken care of by others, there's no need to remember to take out the garbage or the recycling or the compost, or wash dishes, or do laundry, or charge the car, or buy groceries, or pay the mortgage, or water the plants — you get the idea. In such an environment, we have exactly two options: devote ourselves to science, or let the idleness drive us crazy.

I've been keeping myself occupied over the last two weeks by attentively observing the crew. They're genuine professionals who complete their tasks with the ease of people who enjoy working together — rain or shine, lethal pandemic or no lethal pandemic. We owe these three sailors a great debt. Pete, Sandro, and Lionel are our housekeepers, couriers, labourers, plumbers, electricians, and lookouts. They're the ones who keep our situation from descending into total chaos.

You might think that a group of well-educated adults who are luminaries in their respective fields could achieve a modicum of self-sufficiency. Not on this ship. For example, five of us wanted go out for a breath of fresh air one night. It was fun for a few minutes — there's nothing more bracing than the air at minus forty-three degrees Celsius — until we realized that the door wouldn't open. We'd managed to lock ourselves out. After we'd pounded on the frosted window of the common room long enough, Lionel got the message that we were out on the deck freezing to death. But it turned out that the door wasn't locked. The handle was just jammed in the cold. It took a sledgehammer and a blowtorch to open it again. Since then, all such outings need to be noted in a register, along with their planned duration, and we have to inform a crew member who will be staying inside the boat.

Andy admitted to me that he'd spent his first three weeks taking cold showers because he couldn't figure out the bathroom plumbing until he drummed up the courage to ask Pete to explain where he got his buckets of warm water.

The sailors also operate the winch that hoists the bathy-scaphe and its launching platform. They know the location of every last bolt on the ship, along with the correct tool to tighten it. Their effortless rapport reminds me of my cousins. It's nothing specific, just a particular feeling I get around them that I haven't experienced since childhood.

Lionel is small, chubby, and swarthy. He seems to take great pride in his hairy chest, which he keeps prominently displayed by never neglecting to leave open the top three buttons of his navy-blue jumpsuit. I'm guessing that he's Acadian, but he doesn't mention where he's from. Pete is tall, slim, and quiet. He wears his hair in a long grey braid, which gives him a vaguely exotic look. Then there's Sandro, the Don Juan of the trio. My gut tells me he spends hours every day working out in his cabin. Sometimes, as a party trick, he jiggles his pecs for us. And despite the strict rules against shacking up with shipmates, he can't help himself and flirts with all the ladies. It's somehow never offensive though; he's just the perfect gentleman. He does origami too, so we sometimes get back to our workplaces to find little paper flowers or animals sitting there. I suspect he's in love with the beefier of the ship's two machinists.

Those two don't say a word to us. In fact, we barely see them. Their kingdom is the engine room below-decks. The moment one of the pair appears in the cafeteria, they are immediately called downstairs by some alarm. As our ship powers through the ice, these two work day and night making sure the engines don't overheat. The sailors bring them down provisions and beverages of all sorts. The machinists talk about the *Charlie* like a capricious, faithless lover who can only be coaxed into doing what you want with the greatest of skill. But despite their manic pampering, something's always breaking. Apparently, this is just the way of things. Boats break down, and ours is no exception.

Thanks to the powerful diesel-electric transmission, we can break through ice up to four metres thick. But these engines can't run at full power for long. The sheet of ice we're currently mired in is, in fact, four metres thick. But it also stretches more than thirty kilometres in every direction. It all happened fast: in just a few hours, the ice floes engulfed us. The reinforced hull is unbreakable, but we remain imprisoned here until the tidal action cracks the thick crust.

At first I thought our cook was a bit of a slacker. I mean, most of what he's dealing with is freeze-dried, frozen, or canned. He often serves us military rations. I thought he was just too lazy to turn on his stove. That was before he showed me around his kitchen. I saw the collection of herbs, clinging to life in plastic pots under fluorescent lights. Then there are three growth tanks, where you can see animal muscle fibres — chicken, pork, and beef — floating around. The tanks are low-end models. Out of a total investment of $3,716,834,000, the Canadian government spent less than $100,000 on kitchen equipment, including pots and pans. That means growth tanks that have to be manually drained when certain lactic acid levels are reached. Stretching the fibres makes it more tender.

As if that weren't enough, it doesn't take much more than a funny look to clog the filters on these models. All this to say our cook has to spend most of his shift on tank maintenance, just to keep producing our daily protein intake. When I asked why he went to all that trouble, he said he hates tofu with a passion. Soy farming drained the water table in his hometown, causing droughts that forced his family to move. That's how he found himself here, age sixty, in the depths of the Arctic, cooking for a bunch of spoiled brats who kept requesting things like smoked salmon and wine.

Next, he showed me a row of white plastic buckets with the words *cricket flour* scrawled in black Sharpie. The wink he gave me suggested that when he'd had enough of dealing with the complications of raising meat, he'd toss the rest of the provisions into the sea and we'd have to learn to live on a steady diet of insect meal. I looked back at the pork fibres, bathing in milky water that smelled like infants' vomit. The cook opened a compartment and dropped in three spoonfuls of a fine grey powder. He was making dinner.

Captain Hélène Bisque is the ultimate authority on our ship. She makes every decision that counts. Sure, she consults us, but our rights to an opinion are limited. There is a highly political facet to our mission's presence in the Arctic. Russia doesn't recognize Canada's sovereignty over the North. Denmark doesn't either, but the Danes take a subtler approach to Arctic diplomacy. Their scientific delegations have occupied the territory for years.

It took a while for me to realize that every single spot on our mission was subject to intense international negotiations. My government invested massive sums in this research vessel, but not because it cares about the scientific progress of our inventory or preserving biodiversity. This mission will consolidate its expertise and establish its Arctic credibility — that's the real reason for *Charlie*'s existence. Once the mission is completed and we've saved whatever can be salvaged and confirmed and there's no more to be done, then it'll be open season in the Arctic. And they'll come and do what they always do: scrape everything out and pour cement. Even if we did discover some untold wonder, it would never be enough to slow the massacre. No place is sacred. The problem up here — the difficulty of *accessing* resources — has literally melted away. My country dreams of being first in line to greenlight the Arctic for its resource companies.

These ethical and political concerns seemed so important back when our mission kicked off. Russian and Canadian fighter jets were playing chicken, grazing the ice floes at low altitude in a show of force quite impressive to someone who has never known war.

Andy was running a test with a highly sensitive microphone when two F-35s appeared a few dozen metres above us. The ensuing sonic boom damaged the fragile membrane of his device. His headphones were a writeoff. Andy himself lost his hearing for a full twenty-four hours. He still has tinnitus in his left ear. He was, needless to say, pissed off.

And those were the good days. You know, back before the skies fell silent and the news networks started streaming profiles of heavily armed survivalists explaining how they were fully prepared for the collapse of the system. At the start, we scrutinized our every move. Priorities have shifted now. Captain

Bisque is now under a form of pressure no naval officer's manual could prepare her for: commanding our little Fortress of Solitude, strategically located in the safest area in the world.

I've learned that if you're going to sleep in a cabin below sea level, you can't be claustrophobic. I came aboard with the naive belief that mine would have a porthole. No such luck. When the door closes on my sixty square feet of privacy, it's pitch black, day or night. I unplugged the night light because its blue light was too bright.

I don't have to fumble around in the dark because I use my phone's backlit screen. The cabin is so small that if the device accidentally falls on the floor, I can easily find the switch by running my hand along the wall and turning on the overhead light. After several hours in the dark, the contrast is so violent that I'm blinded for several seconds, even if I keep my eyelids closed.

Since dimmers are prone to short circuits, our cabins don't have them. Candles and other open flames are prohibited. This is no place to relax. It's a space for sleep and personal hygiene. And forget trying to live without an alarm clock. In such darkness our instinct is to sleep all the time, like parakeets when you put a blanket over their cage. The single beds aren't exactly uncomfortable. They're okay for sleeping on, but they sure don't make you want to linger. We're not here to hibernate. And it would be a serious challenge for two people to sleep together.

It's November now, and we're very far north. Dawn has barely brushed the horizon when I start to wonder if humanity will survive the first half of the twenty-first century. Winter solstice is coming soon. That will mean several days of darkness. The cafeteria lights are calibrated to emit ten thousand lux. They flood us with lumens over breakfast in an attempt to stave off the light-deprivation depression as we bolt down our scrambled eggs and coffee. No one has hanged themself yet, so I guess it's working.

On board, there's no such thing as silence. We stop noticing the muffled rumbling of the engines until a breakdown forces the machines to stop for a few minutes or hours. The resulting emptiness is deafening enough to wake us from our deepest sleep. We can hear the water running in the pipes and the metallic palpitations of *Charlie*'s frame twisting.

If you happen to be on deck during one of those brief mechanical reprieves, you can hear the ice floes sing. It's hard not to be impressed by the range — sometimes it squeals like a wounded animal, sometimes it snorts like thunder. Not to mention the wind rushing into every nook and cranny of the ship. Then comes a moan, reminiscent of a howling wolf, when it blows loudly, or a faraway whisper, when it fades.

I dream I'm being digested by a massive beast. The smell that floats into the cabins is somewhere between fresh paint and rust. The taste of blood never leaves my tongue. Some olfactory respite is provided by the organic funk of my and my crewmates' skin, since we're more or less locked in these eight-thousand tons of iron and steel propelled by fossil fuel. The dramatic situation and our forced inactivity create a sense of intimacy. And I'm not immune to the urge for a little tenderness as a salve for our anxiety. Especially after a nightmare.

The deserted hallway is bathed in that grey light that never goes out. I dress in a hurry. The risk of having to evacuate the vessel may be low, but it is always with us, a possibility that must be considered. It's drilled into our heads from the moment we set foot on board. Every time you leave your cabin, you should be dressed and ready for the possibility of having to leap into a lifeboat. Red and black jumpsuits hang on hooks all over the vessel in case we forget ours below. But it's still up to us to remember to put socks on.

The need to dress warmly makes us think twice before leaving our cabin. I get the idea of going upstairs for a breath of fresh air, but once the confusion of my bad dream has been dispelled, I remember that a blizzard is raging and the doors have been locked as a precaution. Gusts of wind this strong could pull us overboard.

I find myself at Andy's cabin door. Without really thinking, I knock. In my nightmare, I was becoming invisible, swallowed up in a metal labyrinth that was closing in on me. The door opens immediately. Andy wasn't sleeping. He's wearing an ancient dark-coloured T-shirt whose many holes afford glimpses of pale skin. It's quite a contrast with the multiple layers of clothing we put on when we're working in the drafty lab. The sight of so much skin is disturbing. My coworker's bare arms reveal a vulnerability I never expected in him.

The hallway's harsh lighting is undoubtedly putting all the imperfections of my face into stark relief, but Andy steps aside to let me in. The cabin is bathed in an orange glow. Another T-shirt has been sacrificed to soften the overhead light. This makeshift lampshade is duct-taped to the ceiling. A strange sound texture spills out from a tiny speaker. If it were possible to record the texture of an intergalactic war of feelings, this just might be what it would sound like. Industrial bass and, up above it, some sort of high-pitched whistling and melodic singing. My expression must have betrayed my confusion, because Andy proudly informs me that the musician is "Weddell fucks."

He doesn't say Weddell "seals." Of course, *phoque*, pronounced *fuck*, is French for seal, and as a result is the one marine mammal name etched in the memory of every English-speaker who has ever sat through a French class. Andy explains that on his last trip to Antarctica, he made hours of recordings of Weddell seals underwater. It's his favourite soundtrack. He listens to it whenever he can't sleep.

As a rule, I'm not interested in married men. Andy is the first exception. He couldn't be further from the stereotype of the guy who gets tied down and proceeds to fill his omentum with fatty tissue while his hair slowly falls out. No, Andy has a very straight back and shining eyes, big hands with curved thumbs, and crooked but healthy teeth.

There are photos of his children on his walls — real photos someone has taken the trouble to print on high-quality glossy paper. Both boys look an awful lot like their father. They have his black hair and brown eyes. One is a teenager, and the younger brother must be around ten. He still has his baby fat, while the older one is all acne-ridden skin and bones. A beach vacation, a mountain hike ... There is even a picture with each family member awkwardly holding a lethargic koala.

A woman with a sagging figure, who I can tell is younger than me, stands in the foreground. I can't help staring at her puffy fingers; she must have water retention. She's smiling with that particular smugness of people who know that their family missions are all they need for fulfillment. The light is turned off. The darkness erases these images from across the world. When our hands meet, I notice Andy has taken off his wedding band.

It takes a few seconds to realize I'm awake and my eyes are open in the dark. My head is resting on Andy's shoulder blade. In my left ear, the steady beating of his heart; in my right, the glaring silence of the ship. Was I woken by the fact that the machines stopped making noise? I don't think so. The engines have been idling for days, to save fuel. They let them run a few hours a day to keep the batteries charged, but at night they're silent. That's when I feel it: a continuous, extremely low-frequency vibration, like some cacophonic catastrophe unfolding underwater. The ice is breaking up at last.

8 Dormancy

WHAT HAPPENS in the depths of the ocean is beyond our powers to conceive. Sunlight scarcely penetrates the surface. Below two hundred metres, you enter the Twilight Zone. Ninety percent of ocean fish live between this layer and the ocean floor. And deeper down, below one thousand metres, is the Bathyal Zone. The largest habitat on our planet lies in perpetual darkness.

We're only beginning to understand how the beings who live at these great depths communicate. When we turn off our diving lights, the water scintillates with multicoloured emanations. The light signals of the creatures of the Bathyal Zone are the most widespread form of communication in the known universe, a radically different way of inhabiting, perceiving, and interacting with the world, existing right alongside us. What is it like to be an octopus, whose arms each form part of an autonomous nervous system? What is an environment to a creature who experiences it most vividly through the electrical fields emitted by its prey? What is the meaning of time passing for a seven-hundred-year-old tree or three-thousand-year-old coral?

These fascinating reflections have been the motivating force driving my career. Yet most people, including our decision-makers, are completely indifferent. They can't see beyond the utilitarian value of the technological advances made possible by scientific discoveries. Research on bioluminescence, for them, is valuable for its concrete applications: the use of phosphorescent markers that target cancer cells, ultrasensitive sensors to target precise light spectra, and economical methods of producing light. A landscaping company has even made a fortune selling flower beds with genetically modified plants that turn pink, green, and blue at dusk. I guess I too could have my own laboratory, with windows that open, if I'd just been smart enough to ask the right question after each of my discoveries: *How much is it worth?*

Apart from a few geologists who like getting their knickers in a knot over some dense layers of mud, most scientists prefer to focus on intergalactic space over the depths of the ocean. It took a long time to design a device capable of withstanding the enormous pressure generated by the ocean. We had to protect the cameras, housings, microphones, thermometers, pressure sensors, and other measuring devices from the onslaught of underwater elements, while ensuring they could still yield reliable data. And human nature being what it is, we aren't satisfied with sending probes. No, we feel the need to go down and look for ourselves.

Too bad we're such a fragile species. The conditions of our survival are comically exacting, compared to other "less highly evolved" life forms. Our bodies are ill-equipped to handle temperature changes, let alone fluctuations in the oxygen supply. We're a mass of soft, watery tissue. The pressure would flatten us like pancakes while microscopic species thrive and take over the world.

And when we do manage to dive more than a few dozen metres below the surface, we can't miss a single decompression stop or we risk oversaturating our blood vessels with nitrogen. Wetsuits are fine for studying shallow environments, but to explore the Bathyal levels and get to know the greater depths beyond, there's no option but squeezing into the relative safety of a bathyscaphe.

For all these sundry reasons, I find myself here on the deck of the *Charlie*, at three in the morning, waiting for Mitch and the sailors to perform the final checks before launching *Charlie*'s "Little Diver," our state-of-the-art submersible that is also our oceanographer's pride and joy. Mitch may not have any children, but at least he has his "Little Dee," as he affectionately calls it. I think he'd sleep in it if he could. He visits it every day on the bridge. When the weather is too dangerous for Mitch's daily visit, we know we have to give him a wide berth.

Even I have to admit it though: this little sub is a technological marvel. It's equipped with a panoply of measuring instruments and sophisticated mechanical arms we manipulate with sensor-equipped gloves that precisely report our smallest movements. Everything also comes with glasses connected to 360-degree 3D cameras that let us visualize our actions in real time. It feels almost like we're fish, watching the scene unfold in augmented reality.

A twenty-two-centimetre-thick spherical hull protects the crew from the water pressure. Three tiny portholes have been pierced into the metal. We prefer using the cameras to find our way, but you can never be perfectly safe from technical failure. It would also be hard, psychologically, to spend the hours required for each dive inside a windowless sphere. These portholes aren't much but they alleviate our anxiety. They're made of thick Plexiglas that can handle the pressure variations between the cabin and ocean outside it, where the pressure can be up to four-hundred times greater than on the surface. At this point, we're willing to place our trust in the hands of the engineers who designed the structure, the workers who built it, and of course Mitch, Pete, Sandro, and Lionel, who inspect it right before we set out.

Despite the cold and the torpor that will descend on us in this murky darkness, I turn down the hot coffee my companion offers me. There's nothing worse than fighting the urge to pee in the heart of the Abyssal Zone. All the ship's lights are on. We must be visible for miles around. The sea is calm, waveless. When the conditions are favourable for a dive, you can't miss your chance. The wet snow that has been falling for a few minutes now makes us blink our eyes.

The surfaces have slowly covered over with a thin film of ice. This makes travel risky. So, I stay still, wrapped in layers of down and microfiber. The rest of the team come out to watch our departure, in a show of solidarity, with their arms resting on the rail of the upper deck. Hopping around somehow makes the cold more bearable.

We made our previous dives near the coast, in the spots identified as most promising by previous missions. But something catastrophic must have happened before we got here, because every dive site so far has presented the same scene of desolation.

I remain cautiously optimistic. I'm convinced life didn't just allow itself to die out. For years people believed that nothing could survive in a hostile environment. Then we discovered extremophiles: microorganisms living in seemingly implausible conditions. They've been found everywhere, from the upper layers of the atmosphere to the heart of hydrothermal vents in ocean trenches, where pressure is so high that the water temperature can reach four hundred degrees Celsius without coming to a boil. In the most unusual places, we've found complete ecosystems devoid of solar energy, populated by bacteria that are fed by gases toxic to humans. A scientific consensus is emerging around the theory that life first appeared in such extreme environments. Our earliest ancestors lived in the gates of hell.

There's no doubt in my mind, then, that some of the species must have managed to move around and survive. My ambition is to find them. I've convinced Mitch to let me try a dive off the coast, into very deep water, that will push his beloved craft to its limits. There are, of course, submarines designed to go much deeper than the *Charlie*'s Little Diver. But our mission isn't to explore the Mariana Trench like James Cameron, who hasn't been calling us with offers to lend us his sub. If he's managed to escape the pandemic, he's probably whiling away the days in the bunker of his California mansion.

Our maximum depth is 2,300 metres. It'll be a riskier dive, but also a more exciting one. Our captain agreed to drop anchor very close to a two-kilometre trench with a gentle westward slope. The plan is to follow the rock face to the deepest point and take samples. We have pressurized containers for this very purpose. I won't be able to open them until I get back on dry land, since the only pressurized tank available is in *Charlie*'s laboratory. I'm saving that one for when I capture some large specimen that would need the space to preserve its freedom of movement. I'll still be able to ensure that the survival conditions of the samples are maintained, thanks to the data collected from each biotope. We need these species to survive until our mission's end, a few months from now.

Given the surface area of these great depths, a simple mathematical calculation suggests that beyond the Twilight Zone the variety of corals is greater than in all the shallow oceans covering the globe. Our work is in its infancy. Estimates suggest that less than 5 percent of the seabed has been explored.

Most polar dives lead to discoveries of new species. The same is true of deep-water dives. Or was, at least, until a few years ago. Recent failures are clouding this statistic. When I learned that the objective of a dive deeper than two kilometres had been approved, I pointed out to Henri that more people had been sent into space than witnessed the area we would dive into.

Halotolerant:
How many people in the sub?

EPicFail1996:
Two. Mitch and I.

Halotolerant:
And at Mission Control?

EPicFail1996:
Oh, you mean the corner of the lab? Three. Captain Bisque (commanding officer), Faith (guidance and communications, she likes to stick her nose everywhere), and Rafaella the mechanical engineer (in case of technical problems).

Halotolerant:
Wow! Hahaha … LOL!

EPicFail1996:
What do you mean "LOL"? Obviously, we don't have NASA's budget to hire a hundred flight engineers so we can have three of them monitoring each dial.

Henri's messing with me. I want to tell him that Andy will be nearby, but he doesn't like it when I mention his name. My sex life annoys him. Then our connection cuts out before I can reply.

I only hope no fishing vessels have been trawling within our perimeter. I get the signal to board Little Dee. Mitch is at the control panel with his headset on. As copilot, my role is to touch strictly nothing, unless he suddenly dies. It's already cold. They wish us good luck and lock the door. Mitch and I fall into a feverish silence. We wait while the crane moves the bathyscaphe, which is slowly approaching the surface of the sea, before we are set in the black water. The signal is given, the suction cups come off with a dull noise, and we begin our descent. It's going to be a long dive.

We follow the chain holding one of the two anchors until we reach the bottom. The instruments indicate seventy-five metres. The interior is dark, save the bluish glow of the screens and control buttons. Under Little Dee's lights, the ocean floor looks grey. Once again, it's a desert. We don't linger. After heading west for two-hundred metres, there's a change in elevation. We're descending a slope that's holding steady at around fifteen degrees. We follow it for two hours. We're in no rush.

Grooves appear in the sand. There is evidence of a recent visit from sea urchins. I want to cry with relief. We take a few photos and continue our descent. We've just crossed the two-thousand-metre mark when we hit the jackpot. A dense forest of tubeworms. They're long and slender, swaying in the gentle ocean current like branches in the wind. This colony must be made up of several million individuals, spread out over hundreds of square metres. The bright red of their tips contrast sharply with the rest of their bodies, which look white in the spotlight. The high-definition camera keeps recording. We take a few samples. There are shrimp and clear blue copepods living among the worms. We sample a few decilitres of water.

I can't wait to get this soup under the microscope. We're euphoric. We've found more in four hours than the previous two years of research. We decide, with the captain's approval, to continue exploring. The wind likely won't pick up until evening. The sea is still calm on the surface, and we aren't likely to cross paths with any drifting icebergs.

We've found our way to a large methane deposit. The gas is slowly seeping out from the rock, rising in small bubbles. This must be the food source of the bacteria that live in symbiosis with the worms. None of the creatures here can use photosynthesis to produce the energy they need, and the sea above is too depleted for there to be enough sea snow to fertilize such an abundance of animals.

This means, aside from solar energy, there has to be another source. It must be methane. This gas is crucial to the large concentration of microorganisms we've found. I can already imagine the rush that will develop to exploit the deposit that lies dormant here. Mitch and I will probably be the only ones privileged enough to observe this tiny world before its permanent annihilation. We'll post the footage to YouTube, as part of the grieving process.

But where there's methane, there's often brine too. We often find brine pools in the vicinity of fossil fuel deposits. Their high salinity prevents the waters from mixing with the rest of the ocean, where the salt content is lower. Brine ponds are essentially lakes on the ocean floor. Each is its own ecosystem. I'm sure the tubeworm forest must be sitting on the outskirts of a brine pond, so needless to say I'm raring to go. Mitch tells me to simmer down. We'll systematically survey the perimeter, follow our dive plan. If we run out of time, we can always come back. The readings show a stable elevation, except for a hollow, measuring around fifty metres, not far from where we now find ourselves. Mitch agrees that we can check that out first.

We've been exploring for over an hour when the scenery changes. The forest thins, giving way to the usual greyish sandy soil. In the submersible's beams of light, we see nothing. My disappointment is so apparent, Mitch decides to offer me a little extracurricular experience. First, he makes sure I don't need to grab anything. Then he turns out all the lights inside, including our on-board instruments. It's totally dark. After five minutes, a very faint glow can be seen entering the passenger compartment through one of the portholes.

"Check this out! Not too fast."

Mitch moves away from the porthole so I can look. Off to our left, at a distance that is hard to judge, something is happening. It looks like an underwater aurora borealis. If there weren't already two of us here to witness it, I would swear it was an optical illusion, maybe caused by the imprint left on our retinas by the lights. It's like how you sometimes see spots when you close your eyes. We turn the instruments back on and contact Faith to let her know where we're going. Though she doesn't miss much, she hasn't figured out what we're up to. She probably thinks we turned off the microphones so she wouldn't hear me cry.

A bed of giant mussels surrounds the brine pond, like a rocky beach. Above it hover thousands of small eel-like, light-emitting creatures. There are so many, packed together so thick, that from a distance they create the illusion of a single compact body. Before long, the reason for their presence is revealed. A whale carcass is floating in the brine pool. The part lying above the surface has been gnawed clean down to the bone. A few photos sent to the surface confirm that it's the corpse of a bowhead whale.

Though the message from our Japanese technicians is matter-of-fact, I imagine they must be crestfallen. After all this time, we've found our first whale, and it's dead. Though we sidle up slowly, we still manage to disturb an emaciated Greenland shark. The submarine's electric field piques its curiosity, and for several minutes it inspects the bathyscaphe. We manage to take flesh samples from the corpse of the whale and close-up photos of the scavenger's speckled skin. The parasites clinging to its eyes float along either side of its head like long, faded handlebar ribbons, a clear indication that the shark is blind. It gets back to its meal.

I'm very surprised to see a shark in such a deep pit. It seems to be immune to the brine's toxicity. The shark eats quietly, occasionally lashing its tail to loosen a shred of tallow. Though it's my mission to save endangered species, this shark is too big to capture and keep alive in my pressurized tank. I'd planned to collect surface species, inhabitants of the reefs found near the icy coasts. I made sure I had plenty of water coolers, but I brought very few aquariums fit for abyssal creatures.

And, of course, there's no way to get heavy equipment delivered. Supply runs are unpredictable and restricted to the bare essentials. We don't even know who's in charge anymore. Receiving is onerous, since nothing can be touched until we've made sure it's aseptic and rabies-free. Most of the governments that have managed to hold on to power have been in emergency mode for at least two years. They couldn't care less about us. We still consider ourselves lucky. Some French colleagues of ours had their ship requisitioned for military manoeuvres. We never heard from them again.

I had no idea life had taken refuge so far from us. The sonar indicates a depth of 2,173 metres. I managed to collect a few eels and other samples of the milky soup from the basin and its surface. It's time to go back up now. I'm frozen to the bone and ready for my weekly shower. The return trip takes a long time but goes smoothly. We find ourselves once again in limpid water. It's a clear, lifeless blue.

The biting, dry wind feels like a slap after macerating in a cool humidity for hours. It's daylight, so an orange glow is visible on the horizon. I hear the applause of my colleagues as I suck in deep breaths of fresh air. The sky is cloudy. The ship is surrounded by hundreds of ice blocks. Their silhouettes reflect the oranges, pinks, and purples of the midday dawn. Never have I been so touched by the beauty of the world. My samples will be brought to the lab. I don't need to supervise. I'm too tired to be of help anyway. I choose to rest a few hours before dinner. The adrenaline wears off under the jet of hot water, and I'm asleep before I even pull down my blankets.

The biopsies tell us that the dead whale was female and at least 230 years old. This makes it the oldest bowhead whale on record. There's no way of knowing how long she's been lying in that pool in the ocean floor though, with half her body preserved by the brine and the above-surface half eaten away by unhurried predators in the Arctic waters. At some point she sank here. Her body now feeds a world of its own. I guess it's a better way to go than ending up as a cube of margarine in the 1930s.

Mitch is already planning another dive with our Japanese whale experts. It was cramped enough with the two of us, so I'm hard pressed to imagine three people squeezing into the submarine's cockpit. I'll listen to the communications with a bag of chips.

I try to imagine the world into which this whale was born over two centuries ago. She would have known quieter, richer oceans — that much is certain. We owe so much to these gentle, peaceful giants. They're the ones who paid the ultimate price for our fear of the dark. Despite it all, a few managed to survive in the glacial waters.

Whales live in families. They undertake dangerous seasonal migrations, from the north to the south pole, to feed themselves and offer their offspring the greatest possible opportunity. Mothers often carry their young for over a year, and after giving birth care for their little ones day and night for months and even years.

Since the dawn of time, these social, communicative, yet solitary creatures have been subjected to human presence: they were privy to our first steps in the water, the first strokes of our paddles, the first engines, the first bombs. They've been there listening to the murderous follies we have let ourselves be swept up in, with no regard for them. Still, the coup de grâce wasn't our harpoon guns but our indifference.

Everyone can see the mess we've made, but no one's doing anything to fix it. I'm part of the massacre too. I compile, collect, and save an infinitesimal part of the biodiversity, knowing full well that once I'm gone, it will all be destroyed without remorse. I know it's irrational and pathetic, but I can't shake the thought that this whale may have died of despair.

Now here I am floating above her. A bowhead whale that was already elderly when I came into the world. I can't decide if I'm in the right place at the right time, in the right place at the wrong time, in the wrong place at the right time, or in the wrong place at the wrong time. A series of coincidences led us to her watery grave. All I know for sure is we got here too late.

There's always been a lag between key events and my responses; it's the story of my life. I'm a collector of funereal urns, samples, approximate reconstructions, regrets. My job is to preserve the remains after the tombs have been pillaged. I always show up just in time for the funeral. Try as I may to revive lost worlds, to turn back the clock and freeze my meagre successes in amber, it's an impossible task since life is first and foremost a question of movement.

Ever since I got here, time has been contracting and expanding. The past seems to be right here next to me, a blink of an eye on the cosmic scale. Since family has always been a painful notion for me, I'm surprised to find myself reflecting on my lineage. My parents are long dead, and I never knew my grandparents. In my family we die young. We move away and lose touch with our elders, as it happened in my mother's family. I should have asked my dad more questions, pushed past his reluctance to talk about the sources of his deep grief. I should have pressed him harder, even if it made him uncomfortable.

My father's side of the family is scarcely less of a mystery. My grandfather Onésime Pic was born in Montreal. He was a baker, like his father before him. My grandmother was a housewife. I don't even know her maiden name. Onésime and Thérèse had two children, my father and my aunt Élie. Onésime kicked the bucket in his early forties, and my grandmother took over the bakery. She died when I was still a baby.

In an old shoebox in the back of a closet somewhere there's a faded photo of her holding a tiny, red-faced infant. On the back, in blue cursive: Thérèse and Émeraude, August 1987. This is the only image I have of my grandmother. In profile, the resemblance is clear. But I haven't worked with flour since we made paste in kindergarten. In the space of two short generations, my genetic code shed any trace of a vocation for baking.

Our mission is dragging on, but we really have nothing to complain about. Despite certain deprivations, we've been spared the worst of the crisis while living in relative material comfort. We're doing our best, under the circumstances. Calm will inevitably return. We'll come back with the results of two years of hard work, our little gift to the world.

Yesterday, we anchored near a shallow bay on Baffin Island so Andy could do his work. After missing the previous season, the belugas are back to moult again this year. There are only a few dozen, but they make an incredible racket we can hear even on the bridge. The sun is rising a little higher in the sky every day. It's a bright, cloudless day. While Andy is busy setting up his recording equipment to capture and film the antics of the pod, the rest of the team sets off to explore the bank, rifles in hand in case we come across a hungry polar bear.

I haven't set foot on dry land since we left the Koksoak River. (Sea ice doesn't count.) We've all lost our land legs. We stumble around like drunks leaving the bar and have a good laugh over it. I've read that some people never recover from long stretches at sea. Instead of going away after a few hours on dry land, their sense of being part of an incessant swell stays with them their whole lives. We move forward, in no earthly hurry. The sun warms our faces when the wind drops. Our aim is to reach the plateau, about a kilometre from the coast, to watch the birds nesting in its crags. You have to be careful though, since there are huge ice-filled cracks sheared out of the rock.

Mitch catches sight of a dark spot in a translucent block of ice exposed by the melt. He gets excited, convinced it's a pocket of soil scraped up by the movement of a glacier millennia ago. He's not even a geologist, but he still gets worked up over the slightest thing.

Our team goes back to the ship, in search of equipment. I opt to lounge on the pebble beach where Andy is gathering data. I've never seen belugas this close up before. They're cavorting around in a few feet of water, scraping their thick yellowed skin on the pebbles to leave space for a new layer of skin to emerge. The images that come up on the cymascope are meaningless, except to an electro-acoustician. He tells me they are elevations. The belugas are having a chat about the state of the bay while transmitting three-dimensional images of our surroundings, which the cymascope interprets for us. I guess we can't exactly expect the belugas to produce pictograms of a tree or Michael Jackson or Mount Fuji. Their mental universe isn't the same as ours.

One particular image intrigues me. It's fractured into thousands of tiny points. One of the belugas is either sharing its fantasies of a huge school of fish or letting its thoughts run wild over the spawning habits of cod. I mean, what do *we* talk about when we spend a week at the spa?

Mitch is working a drill, trying to extract a sample of what he hopes is ancient dirt buried in the middle of a block of ice. He sticks needle-nosed pliers into the hole, and we all hold our breath when he pulls them out. What they clasp turns out to be not a handful of dirt, but a clump of black hair.

It takes three days to extract the block of ice. The thing that we're painstakingly exhuming turns out to be a perfectly mummified human corpse. It's greying temples and salt-and-pepper beard tell us he's a middle-aged man. The tattered strips of what was once a thick fur tunic reveal coppery skin that has been tanned by the cold. Even freeze-dried from spending centuries in a block of ice, his arm muscles are impressive. We count seventy-eight deep scars, mottling the skin of his back, cheeks, and forearms, forming a strangely beautiful abstract pattern.

The most spectacular part is the design tattooed on the inside of his right thigh. The black ink lines seem to clearly depict a battle between a sperm whale and a giant squid. I'm not just imagining it, like some prehistoric Rorschach test. The sperm whale's head has been drawn in great detail, and so have the eight tentacles wrapped around the mammal's jaw. Only certain parts of the two creatures fighting are visible, the rest recede under the blurry line representing the sea. Our man must have witnessed this confrontation. At the very least, someone who did gave the tattoo artist a detailed account.

To this day, the existence of such battles is a matter of conjecture. Our only clues are circular scars the size of dinner plates that are sometimes found near the jaws of sperm whales. These we imagine to be traces of squids' suckers. Squid fragments have also been found in the stomachs of these mammals. The eye of a giant squid, measuring forty centimetres in diameter, has been discovered, suggesting the existence of specimens reaching twenty-five metres in length.

These instances of predation between two mighty species take place underwater. There are reports of sailors claiming to have seen these animals fighting on the surface, but their credibility is uncertain. No matter how many cameras we attach to large mammals, no such epic battle has ever been captured on film. A phrase I heard in a documentary once comes back to me: the diver said that he'd been in front of a sperm whale when it made a clicking, which is one of the sounds they use to communicate. It was so powerful "it felt like getting kicked in the chest by a horse."

Our tests show that this prehistoric man had a fractured collarbone and multiple cracked ribs. He appears to have survived these injuries and died years later. The eleven teeth left in his mouth are badly worn. One foot sits snug in a beautifully designed sealskin boot. He must have lost the other during his final misadventure. He is short, 1.52 metres, and stocky. He has prominent cheekbones, and his face is twisted into a grimace that suggests a violent death. All available evidence, including the precision of his tattoos and the number of scars, suggest he was a respected warrior.

We give our ancient friend his own freezer in the kitchen. This doesn't thrill the cook, who claims it's going to give him nightmares. But then, he also makes jokes about throwing him into our stew. Truth is he's been in a foul mood since the second tank conked out. He's been alternating between "chicken" and cricket. Which isn't actually that bad, it turns out. But I still wouldn't say *no* to a pizza with the works.

Moved by an uncharacteristic democratic impulse, Captain Bisque took a moment to see how we were all feeling about taking this little exploratory jaunt while civilization's most vulnerable landmarks were being destroyed. It's bad out there — worse than even the most pessimistic forecasts. A Finnish laboratory has successfully developed an effective vaccine, but hasn't been able to produce it in large enough quantities to turn the tide. Heads of state and key office holders got vaccinated first, followed by medical personnel, academics, and law enforcement officials.

Every country received a set number of doses based on its population, and was free to distribute them as it saw fit. Which meant that before the precious boxes were unloaded from the plane, corruption, bribery, and wheeling-and-dealing were already rife. CEOs got their doses before ministers of justice. Drug lords sauntered to the front of the line ahead of nurses. Portuguese soldiers intercepted packages before they could take off for Africa. To add insult to injury, many of those vaccinated were already infected. No matter how effective the vaccine was in preventing infection, it has no curative effect on people who are unwitting carriers.

The most recent census puts the human population of earth at 417,000, plus the six-person crew of the POO Rocket, who have spent three months in orbit waiting to be picked up with a patched-up SpaceX rocket. That's to say, the virus has killed 99.999 percent of the once eight-billion-strong human race. That's a remarkable success rate for a single virus. But there are still hundreds of thousands of us left.

The peregrine falcon was classified as a "minor concern" by the International Union for Conservation of Nature when there were only seven thousand breeding pairs distributed across North America. Even now we're thirty times more populous than that. Don't worry about us. The extinction of the human race remains far off in the future.

Individually, we've all had goodbyes to say. For example, I've stopped hearing from Tintin. I can't say whether this mission will have a long-term impact on the human race, but my boss likely saved my life when she convinced me to join up. I haven't been able to reach my cousins since I left. Henri is holding tight in his NASA bunker.

Six months ago, the *Charlie*'s entire team of researchers and crew members voted unanimously to prolong the mission. We'd just lost the signal of the last continuous news stream. No one was exactly thrilled to go and jump into the mass grave. We'd rather be cowardly scientists than stupid heroes. The other survivors acted more or less like we did: they did nothing. They isolated themselves and waited for the storm to pass.

> EPicFail1996:
> Riddle for you. First clue: We're soft-skinned organisms that carry an infinite number of worlds inside us.

> SensitiveHannibal:
> The duodenum, jejunum, and ileum?

> EPicFail1996:
> Nope. Second clue: my people sent a gold disc engraved in binary language into the deep void to tell their story to the other inhabitants of the galaxy.

SensitiveHannibal:
Homo sapiens.

EPicFail1996:
Bravo!

A second vote has been held. A drone delivered a small cardboard box that bounced lightly before falling on the bridge and landing in the arms of Lionel, who stood there ready to welcome it with a suspicious glare. Our doses of the vaccine. We'll get to sail home, bury our dead, and repopulate the planet; let the cycle continue. I'll sign up for a dating site. I need to meet new people. I've got a pretty clear sense of what my profile will look like.

Woman. Fertility: A1. Likes: slowness and silence. The sweet smell of gasoline from an outboard motor. The oily breath of marine mammals. Big piles of soft blankets on her bed. Listening to men's heartbeats. Ambition: To be that old woman who spits into newborns' mouths to welcome them and make them immune to the world.

J.D. Kurtness

Acknowledgements

Thanks to Miguelle, Suzanne, and Jean-Sébastien for making it across the swamp, in up to our waists.

My gratitude to François Blais, without your generous help and sound advice I wouldn't be in a position to thank the Canada Council for the Arts for its financial support.

Thanks to the entire team at Éditions de L'instant même, publisher of the original French-language edition of *Aquariums*: Geneviève, Jean-Marie, Hélène, and my merciless reviser, Lyse, who has greatly enhanced the quality of the book you are holding in your hands.